# The
# Four
# Corners
## of the Heart

# The
# Four
# Corners
# of the Heart

*An unfinished novel*

# Françoise Sagan

TRANSLATED BY SOPHIE R. LEWIS

 AMAZON **CROSSING**

Previously published as *Les quatre coins du cœur* by Plon in France in 2019. Edited for French publication by Denis Westhoff. Translated from French by Sophie R. Lewis. First published in English by Amazon Crossing in 2023.

Published by Amazon Crossing, Seattle

www.apub.com

Amazon, the Amazon logo, and Amazon Crossing are trademarks of Amazon.com, Inc., or its affiliates.

ISBN-13: 9781542025874 (paperback)
ISBN-13: 9781542025881 (digital)

Cover design by Kimberly Glyder

Printed in the United States of America

# The
# Four
# Corners
# of the Heart

# FOREWORD

Since I took over my mother's estate in 2007, the publication of many new editions has brought me the further privilege of contributing forewords to these books, entrusted by me to a number of sympathetic publishers: *La Vitesse* (Speed); *Bonjour New-York*; *Chroniques 1954–2003*; *Françoise Sagan, ma mère*; and, most recently, *Toxique* (Toxic), in a restored version of the original edition.

The publishers found me something of a sitting duck, indeed a duck that invariably delighted in diving into each new writing task—and I should add that this contribution being to my mother's oeuvre made no difference: the exercise would have been as joyful without that.

Of course, these texts I was presenting had already been edited and in some cases re-edited, had therefore been reread and revised and, most likely, so thoroughly introduced already that it did not make much difference if this last little opinion piece of mine passed entirely unnoticed.

So when Editions Plon asked me to write the introduction to *The Four Corners of the Heart*, I was not surprised, simply gratified by the trust once more placed in me. Only that evening, back home and with time for reflection, did I understand the magnitude of what I had just agreed to do: it consisted, neither more nor less, of presenting a never-published work by an iconic author, the impending first publication of which promised to cause a simultaneous literary typhoon and media earthquake.

Truth be told, I have only the vaguest recollection of how this manuscript came into my hands. It must have been two or three years after I took charge of the estate. The moment this manuscript was passed to me, I felt its existence was nothing short of a miracle, all my mother's belongings having already been seized, sold, given away, or dubiously acquired by third parties.

Although slim, the book's pages were bound only by a plastic cover—the kind students use for publishing their theses—and it consisted of two volumes. The first was entitled *Les quatre coins du cœur* or *The Four Corners of the Heart*, and the second, which opened with "The Paris train came into Tours station at 4.10 pm . . . ," was called *Le cœur battu*

(The beaten heart). At that time there was no definitive title for the novel and, as I write these lines, I still don't know which we will choose.

The typed text had been photocopied so many times that the letters were no longer quite clear. Crossings-out, annotations, and corrections by unknown hands had been carried out with varying intensity through the two volumes, which had been discovered mislaid amid a stack of files, documents, and other records, so it took me a while to realize this was all part of a single novel.

So it was, by a series of lucky—or rather, unlucky—coincidences, that at first I paid little attention to this manuscript. I had no notion it could be an unpublished novel. Besides, my mother's estate was in a state of deep disorder, and my thoughts were exclusively occupied with disentangling apparently inextricably knotted legal, fiscal, and editorial issues.

Nonetheless, looking back to that moment now, I was strangely casual about this text that, although unfinished, had astonished me with its powerfully Saganesque style—the often wickedly sharp portraits, the baroque tone and fantastical nature of some of the plotting—so I must have been careless indeed to pay it so little attention, to the extent of leaving *The Four Corners of the Heart* in a bottom drawer over the intervening years. But its unfinished nature appeared such that it would have been unwise to share the book with any reader I didn't absolutely trust.

A few months earlier, I had done the rounds of most of Paris's publishers, who, with their successive rebuffs, had led me to fear that Françoise Sagan's works would vanish along with the final hours of the twentieth century. And then I met Jean-Marc Roberts, the man for my hour of need, who later became my mentor on editorial questions related to the estate. At the time, he was director of the publisher Editions Stock, and one April afternoon he agreed on the spot to republish every one of the fifteen of my mother's books that I'd brought to his office on rue de Fleurus. Besides his becoming my publisher, I rapidly came to consider Jean-Marc my friend, so it was naturally to him, a few weeks later, that I confidentially entrusted the reading of this novel whose muddled condition nonetheless left no doubt as to its potential publication.

*The Four Corners of the Heart* had already, previously, been the subject of a film adaptation—hence the endless photocopies—although this project never reached our screens. The manuscript had therefore been modified, even substantially reworked, in the hope of inspiring a then-fashionable screenwriter. As it turned out, *The Four Corners of the Heart* could not be published in this state, for its patent weaknesses could have done real harm to my mother's oeuvre.

The idea of having the novel revised by some contemporary author equal to the task did occur to Jean-Marc and me.

But the manuscript as it was, missing words here and there, occasionally even whole passages, was so compromised by these gaps that we soon abandoned the idea.

The text was returned to a back burner, which did not prevent its being read again several times, each time more attentively, over the next few months. Several voices intimated that I was the only person who could revise the book, and that the novel *had* to be published, whatever its state, because it would restore a fundamental piece, however imperfect, to Françoise Sagan's oeuvre. Those who knew and loved Sagan ought to have access to her entire literary output and be able to appreciate the accomplishment of everything she wrote.

I set to work once more, carrying out the corrections I felt were necessary while taking care not to affect the style or tone of this novel in which I rediscovered, as I went on, the utter freedom, the untrammeled wit, the dry humor, and the audacity bordering on insolence that characterize Françoise Sagan.

Sixty-five years after *Bonjour Tristesse* and ten years into a troubled afterlife, *The Four Corners of the Heart*, Sagan's incomplete final novel, is published at last and in its most authentic, unadorned form: an indispensable gift to all her readers.

Denis Westhoff

# 1.

Framed by four great plane trees and furnished with six benches in racing green, the terrace at La Cressonnade was majestic. And the old pile must once have been a fine old provincial residence, but it was no longer either beautiful or even really old. Recently decked out with additional pinnacles, various external staircases, and further wrought-iron balconies, the house brought together two centuries of expensive bad taste that undermined the sunshine, the trees, the slate gray of its gravel, and all its verdant surroundings. The perron, formed of three flat gray steps, was finished with a medieval-style balustrade—the final cherry on top of this unsightly concoction.

But the two people sharing a bench that faced the house, one at either end, seemed untroubled by it. Ugliness can be easier to look on than beauty or harmony, which we spend all our time double-checking and admiring. In any case, Ludovic and his wife, Marie-Laure, appeared as unmoved as anyone could be by this architectural bedlam. Moreover, they weren't looking at each other, nor at their house; they were focused on their feet. However beautiful their shoes, there's something broken about people who seek neither a face nor a façade to rest their eyes on.

"You're not cold?"

Marie-Laure Cresson turned to her husband inquiringly. With her pretty face—expressive mauve eyes, faintly posed mouth, and ravishing nose—she had made many conquests before marrying, rather hurriedly as it happened, this hale and vigorous young man known as Ludovic Cresson, himself something of a playboy and something of a fool, over whom the young women of the sixteenth arrondissement had been scrabbling in view of his fortune and his cheery style. Although notoriously crazy about women, Ludovic Cresson would make a loyal husband, this was clear. Alas, almost all his qualities—apart from his wealth—were faults to Marie-Laure. Sophisticated, light on education but, thanks to a grab bag of fashionable reading and a handy polish of buzzwords and taboos, she was known to her circle as a quick and perfectly attuned intelligence. She intended to run her own life, and therefore others' lives too; she meant to "live her life," as she herself expressed it. But she had no idea what life was nor what she wanted from it, unless that was luxury. In fact, she wanted to be enraptured. However expensive her jewelry and however wealthy Henri Cresson, Ludovic's father (known as the "Hawk on High" in his native region of Touraine), she would be ready to flaunt them.

◆ ◆ ◆

We shall not explain—for obvious reasons—why the old factory and the great walls of the house were named La Cressonnade. Furthermore, it would be complicated, and even more tedious, to explain how the Cressons themselves made their fortune out of watercress, chickpeas, and other diminutive vegetables, which they nowadays distributed to the farthest reaches of the planet. This uninteresting subject would demand, at least in the case of your author, more imagination than memory.

"Are you chilly? Would you like my sweater?"

The voice of the man at Marie-Laure's side was naturally gentle and pleasant, albeit too questioning and too vulnerable given the insignificance of the question. Besides, the young lady fluttered her lashes and turned away, thus indicating a kind of subtle disdain for her husband's sweater (which she had scrutinized in the space of a second).

"Oh, no, thanks. I'll go back in; it'll be easier. You ought to do the same. This isn't the moment to catch a cold as well."

She stood and made for the house at an untroubled pace, gravel crunching under her fashionable shoes. Even in the country, even quite alone, Marie-Laure exhibited elegance and the latest style, no matter the occasion.

Her husband watched her with an admiring and also somewhat mistrustful gaze.

◆　◆　◆

It should be said that Ludovic Cresson had only just emerged from a series of sanatoriums, to which he'd been consigned by a road accident so disastrous, so horrific, that neither his doctors nor his lovers could have dreamed he would survive.

With Marie-Laure at the wheel, the little sports car he'd bought for her birthday had been crushed against a parked truck and the passenger side torn off by the steel bars the lorry had been carrying. While Ludovic's head had been extracted aesthetically intact, and while Marie-Laure had come out untouched of face or body, Ludovic's body had been gored in several places. He had gone into a coma and the doctors had given him a day or two, maximum, to take his leave of this mortal coil.

Except that, within the natural fortress of his body, the shoulders, neck, and lungs and other organs making up the outer and inner health of this naïve boy turned out to be much smarter and more tenacious than anyone imagined. So while thoughts were turning to ceremony and funeral music—while

Marie-Laure was assembling a soberly superb outfit of widow's weeds (very simple, with a purposeless bandage at her temple); while Henri Cresson, furious at his procreative project's stalling, was kicking every object in sight and insulting his domestic staff; and while his wife, Sandra, Ludovic's stepmother, cultivated her habitual overbearing dignity as an often bedbound invalid—Ludovic himself fought back. And at the end of the week, to general consternation, he awoke from the coma.

As we know, some doctors can be more attached to their diagnoses than to their patients. Ludovic exasperated all the big shots Henri had (naturally) summoned from Paris and everywhere else. The ease with which he returned to life so irritated them that he was found to have something potentially very compromising on the brain. This—and his own silence— was enough to consign him to close observation and then to a more specialized health facility. He was befuddled, so appeared somewhat vacant—even to have suffered some brain damage— and the perfect vigor, the very healthiness of his body only reinforced this impression.

For two years, wordless and unprotesting, Ludovic went from clinic to clinic, from psychiatric unit to psychiatric unit, and was even sent to America, literally strapped down inside his jet. Every month, his little family would visit to watch him sleep—or to "smile stupidly at him," as they muttered among themselves—before leaving again at top speed. "I cannot bear the sight," Marie-Laure moaned, not even trying to hold back a false tear, for, in their car, all were decidedly dry-eyed.

Not all: the exception was Marie-Laure's mother, the very charming and recently widowed Fanny Crawley, still mourning her husband when she came to see the son-in-law she had not appreciated before. Ludovic's devil-may-care, cowboyish style had got on the nerves of many, many sensitive women, even while it had also tickled many, many decidedly spirited women. So it was that she returned to see the man she'd called a playboy prostrate, strapped down at the wrists and ankles, grown dreadfully thin and somehow much younger too, looking as harmless as he was vulnerable and quite incapable of refusing all the psychoactive drugs being fed into his veins from dawn to dusk . . . and Fanny Crawley had wept. She'd wept until Henri noticed and drew her aside for a serious and private conversation.

Happily, Henri Cresson had then managed to speak to the director of that latest clinic—possibly the most expensive of its kind in France and certainly the most useless. The head doctor had told him categorically that his son would never, ever recover. Now, certainty in others invariably provoked disbelief and rage in Henri, who was as brilliant at business as he was hopeless at emotions (not having had any, or rather having had them only for his first wife, Ludovic's mother, who had died in childbirth). He had been, then, stunned to see this beautiful and elegant young woman, whom he knew to be inconsolable over the loss of her husband, weeping over a son-in-law she disliked. Fanny demonstrated persuasively that it was time to stop the torture. Henri had gone back to the doctor and spoken to him in such a way that, despite his institution's eye-watering rates, the latter could no longer retain a patient whose family so scorned his services.

A month later Ludovic arrived at La Cressonnade, where, having thrown his little vials of medicine one after the other into the wastebasket, he turned out to be perfectly fine. He was sweet-tempered, a mite distant, a mite anxious, and did a lot of running. In fact, he spent most of his time running in the vast estate park, running like a child who'd recovered the use of his legs, if not one trying to regain an approximately adult demeanor. There was no question—and indeed there never really had been any question—of Ludovic working in his father's factory: he had wealth enough even without finding a profession discreet enough to justify a life spent in all the best spots around Europe (the life Marie-Laure very much meant to lead, with or without him).

Ludovic's return was a disaster for Marie-Laure. She had been admirable as his widow, but finding herself the "wife of an idiot," as she cast herself among her closest friends (who shared a very public social life), was quite another thing. Marie-Laure began, then, to hate this boy whom she had previously put up with and even vaguely liked.

Still, Ludovic's former raptures, his love and passion for her, would rapidly have annoyed Marie-Laure. For Ludovic had loved women passionately; he loved romantic love as perhaps the only art he practiced with skill and care. Ardent and gentle, he had been charming—and all the (very many) whores of Paris who knew him from before still harbored deep affection for him.

Under the sole supervision, then, of the village doctor, Henri Cresson's man, Ludovic was recovering very nicely. Although modest, this doctor had been proclaiming since the accident that his patient was shattered, exhausted, broken, but in no way insane. And, indeed, no one could detect the least sign of nervousness or any other functional or psychological irregularity in him. Quite simply, not one sign of vulnerability or interest in the future could be detected in him. He was expecting something of which he was afraid. But what? Or who? No one really troubled themselves about this, however, for no one in this house was truly concerned with anyone—other than themselves.

Upon reaching the first step of the ridiculous little perron and laying a languid hand on one balustrade, Marie-Laure was forced to leap to refuge on the highest step, for a racing car guided by a sure hand had just braked right at her feet, creating a broad surge of gravel, which would have made her start or scream had anyone other than her father-in-law been at the wheel. For some time, Henri Cresson had been convinced that his driver was getting old and that he himself should take up driving again—a nightmare for his neighbors and a source of terror for all animals and relatives who encountered him on the road.

"My God, Father," Marie-Laure exclaimed coolly, even so. "Where is your driver?"

"Appendicitis! Resting up," replied Henri gaily, stepping out of the car. "Appendicitis . . ."

"But that makes his fourth bout this year."

"True, but he's delighted. All his welfare benefits, et cetera, and his salary on top: that man is decidedly thumbing his nose at the rest of us and will happily stay in bed as long as required, so afraid is he of the cops, the benefits police, and Lord knows who else."

"You're the one who should be afraid."

"Me, afraid? Of what? Go on, my dear daughter-in-law, do go on."

She hated him calling her his "dear daughter-in-law," but he used the title liberally despite the reproaches of his wife, the redoubtable Sandra, who had come as far as the perron steps to offer her husband a pleasant welcome; usually she kept to her rooms.

Sandra Cresson, née Lebaille, had one fundamental concern: duty. Henri Cresson's neighbor since forever, both in terms of her acreage and her fortune, she had married this widower reputed for dourness out of pure fear of spinsterhood. She had thought she was wedding a somewhat brusque industrialist, but Sandra's husband turned out to be a frenzied bull of a man without the least interest in society life, to her great chagrin. She had hoped to entertain in the vast salons at La Cressonnade but had instead been obliged to concentrate on avoiding her husband's whirlwind comings and goings in the unspeakable drawing room. And this with the knowledge that, before Sandra's reign, other first ladies had made their marks.

Henri Cresson's two brothers had been killed in the battle of 1939–40 ("We had big balls in that battle," Henri would say, cheerily. "Fourteen to eighteen made the heroes, but thirty-nine to forty!"), and their widows had then swiftly moved away, terrorized by their brother-in-law, who, furthermore, allotted both of them generous sums so he'd be left in peace. But they'd still had time to decorate the reception rooms and some bedrooms, which turned this already bizarre house into an almost unimaginable collision zone: between one lady's Moroccan chimneys and the other's Spanish inclinations, and then the marble exclamation marks installed by Sandra (indulging her passion for Greek aesthetics), nobody would have dared to photograph this salon.

Sandra had personally discovered a sculptor in the village of La Cressonnade, a man until then assigned to the graveyard's hoary funeral statuary, whom she had abruptly pitched into the antique artistic world of classical Greece and Rome, his new brief being to copy, to varying specifications and to order, the Venus de Milo and the Winged Victory of Samothrace, works that Sandra ranged in the enormous drawing room as so many defiances or perhaps complaints. Herself more akin to the statuesque than to human dimensions, rounded, solid, and imperturbable in all situations, Sandra Cresson could have stood among her statues from dawn to dusk without anything distinguishing her from them, clothing aside.

"Ah, my wife arrives—the full complement!" Henri exclaimed, tearing a shocking scarf from his neck.

"I don't see what's so surprising about that," Marie-Laure said.

"It isn't your being here, neither the one nor the other of you, that surprised me," Henri replied firmly. "It's that I'm still alive and kicking, between two such, such . . . how can I put it? Two such vivacious—that's the word—such vivacious women."

"Are you not vivacious yourself?" Reaching for this sarcasm, Marie-Laure's voice had achieved a particularly grating pitch.

Leaving the two furious women behind, Henri made rapidly for the awful drawing room, only just skirting a suitcase abandoned in the middle of the room, which he gave a neat kick as he passed.

"What's that doing there?"

"It's my brother's, would you believe, dearest? My brother, Philippe, who has come to stay for a few days."

"And here indeed is dear Philippe himself," Marie-Laure said.

Henri Cresson's numerous defects were really virtues in absence: while he wasn't exactly mean, he never thought of being kind; while not really greedy, he never thought to be generous; and he acted with absolute indifference to others' opinions. In fact, he was rather hospitable by nature, and he found the presence of a man, a true man—for his son seemed to him more like an angel or a ghost—vaguely comforting.

"Good old Philippe. When did we last see him? Ah yes, three weeks ago. I do hope he's well and untroubled by any 'romantic' strife."

Henri's distinctly quote-marked "'romantic' strife" was followed by a peremptory guffaw with which he vanished into the drawing room, leaving the two exasperated women behind.

◆  ◆  ◆

Henri had married Sandra very soon after the death of his first wife, of whom it was known that he'd loved her, although he never spoke of her nor apparently ever tried to console himself. He had "honored" Sandra, in the word's conjugal sense, for a fortnight but had rather forgotten about her after that, and these days he paid tribute to her only occasionally. Being of delicate health, Sandra was relieved by the infrequency of his attentions.

Of course, from the beginning there had been no lack of women in this corner of Touraine to alert Sandra to her husband's straying. But, curiously, despite their number and their maximal fussing, Henri had never imposed the knowledge or the general recognition of his conquests on his wife. He would "go up to Paris," as we used to say, and come back fresh and without comment. It was the least he could do, he thought, for a woman whom he absolutely could not truly honor.

This was also his only bond with his son. When the latter "went up to Paris," as we used to say, it was in the pointless pursuit of business studies, however laudable; Ludovic's complete ignorance of women at age eighteen was due to his isolation and the school where he'd been locked away with other unlucky country boys. Now, this total ignorance of such relations had rather troubled his father. Especially as, two months in, Ludovic began to receive erratically addressed florists' bills, which had the poor boy petrified. Ludovic might be stupid enough to have some little affair with a Parisian girl and get her pregnant or Lord knew what more. So his father now made his way to the capital and discovered to his great surprise that the flowers, all the bouquets and related efforts, were strictly for the different prostitutes in the habit of providing their favors to his son. Relieved but nonetheless concerned about his only child's intellectual health, this time Henri explained to Ludovic that this was not how things should be done. Then, over lunch, he had pondered why indeed it wasn't the done thing, why he himself did not send flowers to the women who had welcomed his advances instead of sending them to the girls from good families who had refused him.

"Oh—do what you wish!" he had declared, in the end.

Delighted, Henri's offspring then kept up his pleasant manners. It was only later on, upon meeting Marie-Laure, that he became unhappy: in love and miserable, more concerned with the life of another than with his own—although less unhappy about not sharing his beloved's life.

Marie-Laure did not hold love, as such, in particularly high esteem, at least not as high as her self-esteem. And yet her own parents, Quentin and Fanny Crawley, had always loved each other and offered an example of faultless intimacy, passion, and affection. But Marie-Laure appeared to despise them for it. Indeed, they seemed instinctively to keep out of her way, even to fear her.

Quentin's death in an airplane accident had crushed Fanny Crawley's spirit. She disappeared from society, her face took leave of her body, the joy vanished from her voice, and her own life seemed to evaporate. Short of money and so obliged to work, thanks to well-placed friends she was hired by a fashion house where, little by little, her natural friendliness, her kindness, and her attention to others established her in a position to feed her daughter and herself. But this wasn't enough for Marie-Laure, and so, suddenly, Ludovic became intriguing.

If Ludovic saw no connection between the two events—the death of one and the other's interest—that was because he did not wish to see it. Even if Fanny did look away when he asked for her daughter's hand; even if his friends changed the subject and congratulated him the way you do someone leaving for distant shores, Africa for example, on military service; he could only wake one day and change his mind then. All this he sensed but gave no thought, for he was madly in love. And at that moment, Marie-Laure was intelligent, or canny, enough to pay him all due attention, to make sure she kept him and no other girl or woman could lay a finger on the sweet, vulnerable, rich, and idle Ludovic Cresson. Deprived of affection from birth, deprived of women throughout his youth, he truly was a man ripe for the plucking; he dreamed of love like a ridiculous Tristan from the previous century.

But the free-spirited ways that guaranteed Ludovic's success among many of his friends also guaranteed Marie-Laure's utter and conclusive contempt. Life was a battle. One of the two would have to lead the charge, and that would be her—alone. Physical love disgusted, bored, and frightened her, despite her lover's very best efforts—his ardor, patience, and gentleness, born of dreams that he and Marie-Laure could be like his parents: a couple shaped in mutual sustenance, a couple of halves like Plato's apple, together a perfect whole.

# 2.

The staircase echoed to a dancing tread: one step, tap, two steps, tap-tap, the landing, tap-tap tap-tap; it seemed youth was descending, and whistling (a happy harbinger, this, for it was a Fred Astaire tune) was floating down with it. Two floors lower, and youth had gained thirty years. It was Philippe Lebaille, Sandra's charmer of a brother who, after a long career of seduction and sponging, could ever more often be found sojourning with his brother-in-law, Henri; although Philippe had always hated the country, over the last five years he had managed not to mention that.

He was a handsome man—at least, he had been handsome and would never forget it (with pride or regret, depending on the day). Tall, slim, twinkle-toed, and virile, Philippe had recently been lucky to find that his Errol Flynn moustache had spontaneously thinned away, thus sparing him an outdated style slavery but leaving behind his habit of coolly stroking the

points despite their having vanished. At twenty-two and handsome then; rich, well-bred, and pretentious; Philippe Lebaille
had been propelled into the rarefied worlds available to his
kind of man by the silly besotted women of *le jet set*. He had
spent his inheritance without ever sharing it; he had seduced
women without ever loving them; for years he had been invited
everywhere but seen nothing apart from palm trees, palaces,
and ski pistes. So, for the last five-odd years, he had been
retracing the steps of his sentimental journey, which he felt
had simply happened to him like a gift, though he was now
leaving that path at some speed as if to avoid a bad memory. In
any case, here he was, pathetic and smiling and posing for some
invisible photographer, just as in the photo that followed him
from house to house, from mirror to mirror, showing him in
Hollywood proudly posed between John Wayne and Marlene
Dietrich. This portrait might have been his most prized possession, apart from a few gold watches and a collection of Indian
shawls as threadbare as they were (once) gorgeous.

"*En famille! En famille* at last!" Philippe exclaimed, coming
to join Sandra and Ludovic.

He gave the latter a friendly but circumspect glance. His
nephew's madness did not bother him, being in his view an
open secret fully recognized by his sister, the mistress of the
house.

"You do look wonderfully well, Ludovic!" he cried, affect-
ing something between delight and surprise.

Ludovic smiled wearily. "Thanks," he said.

"What a joy to see you!" And with her next breath, Sandra exclaimed, turning to her brother: "You're so good-looking!"

Philippe's looks being his only capital, albeit diminishing with every visit, she had to mention them.

"Ah, here you are at last," she added, spotting Marie-Laure, who was, in her turn, floating down the staircase, in the same dress as that afternoon but embellished for the evening with a brooch Ludovic couldn't recall paying for—but his thoughts remained in flux on this point.

Philippe cast a glance at the jewelry of his niece by marriage, then at Ludovic, and, finding only two unextraordinary people, merely smiled.

Henri Cresson's arrival disturbed the tableau.

"My dear Sandra, would you find it very troublesome if we were to dine early? You see, for one thing, I am tired and hungry, and for another, I absolutely must see the debate on TV between this chap from the trade union and someone from the management—I predict sparks will fly," he said, with the sarcastic edge he affected whenever politics came into the conversation.

"Of course, of course, let's see—everything is ready. We'll sit down together right away. Martha will be here in a moment."

The chaos of his drawing room had never bothered the master of the house, but he was disinclined to ford a sea of obstacles in order to reach his goal. Therefore a kind of corridor had been created for his use, a narrow but clear channel to his study at the far end of the room, from which even the smallest figures and furnishings had been removed. Without this measure, the slightest straggler of an object risked ejection by a vigorous kick and the little Moroccan pouf would next be found perched on top of a Gothic chest.

At the end of this channel was the dining room, the study with his private television. The room featured a kind of platform with a table on it, laid for five diners, and five leather armchairs, each of which one could turn right around, its back to the chimney, for full enjoyment of a patently personal television nestled against the French window only two meters away. In the other direction, naturally, Henri Cresson was obliged to face his family over dinner, after which the cloth would be removed and the table relaid with the fax machine and other various objects indispensable to the man of business, however countrified.

Henri set off at a brisk pace, covered the eight meters to his little "study lounge" at a lick, tossed his briefcase onto a spare armchair, and sat down in his own. This was the dining room as chosen, as *designed*, by him. Henri seated the two men opposite and the women on either side of him. Then, as soon as the meal was over, he could swivel around and watch his television in peace, as he had visibly been hankering to do. Naturally, the program he selected was never the one the others requested. Henri preserved a psychological aloofness that offered respite from the inevitable inanities exchanged over dinner. And during this dinner, our patriarch calmly and philosophically concluded, at several points, that his son probably *had* lost his marbles, that his daughter-in-law was worldly and witless, that his wife was ugly and an imbecile, and that he gloried, too, in a moronic parasite of a brother-in-law! A lot in life that he accepted serenely with, just now and then, fits of unpredictable and unseemly fury.

Everyone sat down quickly—which still did not prevent a degree of poise, especially from Marie-Laure, displaying the brand-new brooch her father-in-law hadn't even noticed. Sandra was hardly seated before starting on her routine as the American housewife from all the worst films:

"Goodness, my poor darling, truly you must be dead tired! You do realize how it must feel for a man to spend his day with all these terrible businesspeople and then, all of a sudden, come back to the house and a family of our caliber? Such incredibly different worlds! It's quite enough to exhaust a man."

She directed an affectionate smile at her husband, who, without looking up from the inevitable soup at last before him, only mumbled, "I'm not seeing ferocious enemies all day, my dear Sandra, only a few lazy fools. It's not the same thing.

Indeed, being able to escape here after all the number-crunching is really quite nice."

At this Marie-Laure gave a high-pitched squeak and made a face like a character from an old picture postcard.

"It's what they call the soldier's repose, isn't it, Sandra?" she said, and her mischievous little correction made Philippe want to giggle and had Sandra blushing even as she looked away (she was not sorry she had left her room to be with the rest right now) and, as usual, left Ludovic unmoved.

Blanching slightly, Marie-Laure bore her father-in-law's suddenly frosty glare without flinching.

"Do you know who I once met in the street?" Sandra exclaimed all of a sudden, sensing a storm brewing without understanding where it had blown in from. "I met our Queen of France!"

There was a silence and, looking aggrieved—for Sandra's foolishness was really becoming too much—Henri asked her to repeat this.

"One day I saw the Queen of France in a street in Tours. You know perfectly well that Madame de Boyau was a Valois. Then the Bourbons came and they took all the titles and gave them away to all kinds of people. Now, Madame de Boyau is directly descended from Count . . . I don't remember his name, but he would ordinarily have claimed the throne in just a few steps. Therefore—had there not been all those Bourbons—the true heir and figurehead of France would have been . . ."

Gone a soft shade of violet, she made vague gestures—no longer able, it seemed, to follow her own imputations.

"There must have been a few contributing circumstances aside from the Bourbons' sneakiness, don't you think?" replied Philippe, grinning. "You of course know how to curtsey to the Queen—you had that training as a teenager—but I assure you there must have been other obstacles to her accession."

"And lucky ones!" Henri said, digging into his bread. He'd had enough of this family. "Of course there were other obstacles. Just picture that little lady, Madame de . . . What was her name again? What did you say her name was, Sandra? That little woman who's such a peasant you can even tell from behind! And you want to push *that* on all French people in possession of a television?"

"Come now," she replied, shrugging. "That's luck, just bad luck. Why shouldn't it be her? She's as good as that countess of Paris we have now. It would be nice if the Queen of France turned out to be one of us."

"There was the small impediment of the French Revolution," Ludovic pointed out.

Before the stunned expressions of the other four guests, he realized his error and, raising a hand as if in defense, clarified, "I just thought of mentioning that—adding it to the mix, as it were."

An awkward silence followed, punctuated by each participant's ultimately abortive attempts to restart the conversation.

"Did you go for a walk?" Henri asked, startling his son.

"Yes, Father. I actually went all the way to the ponds. Those old ponds at Carouve, you remember them? It was super."

"We don't see a hair of him from dawn to dusk; that's just how it is," Sandra remarked, shrugging again. And then, for all to hear: "He has no rational faculties at all, neither brain nor memories."

"Well, it's a lot better than him going off to get sozzled in Tours with a bunch of lowlifes," Henri said, with a brief smile in his son's direction, though the latter unfortunately missed it and drifted back into his usual distracted state until his name came up again.

"As for you, I suppose you stayed in bed all day, making phone calls and playing the lady of leisure," Henri accused his wife. "Around here only Ludovic gets anything done at all, with his little walks."

"But I'm afraid he's seen every nook and cranny of your estate by now," Philippe said. "I don't know what he can be up to, unless there's some young shepherdess pining for him out there."

"There are no more shepherdesses," Henri snapped, meanly. "If there were, he'd not be the only one out for such strolls. And what about you, Marie-Laure? Why don't you go with him on these strolls? You never do seem to go too."

"I don't much like strolls, I will admit."

"Haven't you gone with him even once since he came back, a month ago?" Henri asked.

"A month and a half, yesterday," Marie-Laure said. "I left Paris on July seventh, and I'd already come up from the Côte d'Azur to join you. That makes exactly forty-seven days."

Her sour tone lent those forty-seven days a wearisome and distinctly unhappy cast. An awkward silence fell over the table, broken once more by Sandra, as wise mistress of the house.

"But now I think of it," she said, "we absolutely must send out our invitations for the ball, I mean, to celebrate the return of our prodigal child, don't you think? Remember, we had decided it would be at the end of September and we had even selected the date, and now I've forgotten it. Dear God! I've a head like a sieve, I truly do," she added, shaking the faulty part and for a moment abandoning her proud posture.

◆　◆　◆

The second Madame Cresson had relied on the fine carriage of her head to ensure her priorities and her flirtations were met. "The most important thing in a woman," she often said (more and more often, in fact, for she retained very few other distinguishing features, apart from twenty superfluous kilos), "is the fine bearing of her head, her dignity; something unmoving that makes all around defer to her. It is a woman's weapon and her defense all in one, believe me."

Exasperated, Henri had once remarked that it wasn't how one carried one's head but what was inside it that mattered.

"Why," he had even gone on to say, "make so much of an empty vessel?"

"Say what you like, Henri; a woman's neck, shoulders, and nape display both her breeding and her dignity," Sandra had retorted.

And with another shrug of his bullish shoulders, he had closed the conversation, saying, "Let each man bear what he can."

"We'll get started tomorrow, right, Marie-Laure? We shall have three hundred invitations to write. I'm not sure you realize quite how many that is."

"Don't forget all the shepherdesses," Philippe teased. "They must be invited too!"

He was doing his best to inject a bit of spirit, some laughter into the proceedings, but the mood was against him.

"Do you think he would invite them, even if there were any?" Marie-Laure asked, sarcastically. "Anyway, as long as he's not pushing them into the ponds, we shan't go complaining."

Her expression became one of infinite patience.

Since the accident, the Cressons had got out of the habit of using Ludovic's name, the real Ludovic being effectively dead to them. So they called him "he" and said whatever they liked about him as if he wasn't there, even when he was right there. Besides, Ludovic always had an eye wandering elsewhere, on the countryside beyond the windows.

Henri looked at Marie-Laure, then suddenly drawled, "My dear Marie-Laure, you have a fine nose for precision: Could you tell me what the time is?"

"It is almost twenty past eight," she replied, though she did not meet her father-in-law's eyes.

"Thank you so much," Henri said. "You will excuse me. I absolutely must follow the debate; I wouldn't miss it for anything. Thank you. See you later."

◆　◆　◆

He spun coolly around, turning his back on the family, sitting there, spoons in hand before their desserts; picked up the remote control; and turned on the television. After a couple of seconds of crackling interference followed by the weather forecast, his program came on.

Halfway between the Moroccan and the Finnish lounges, there was another television for the rest of the family, so they all gathered on the Chinese-style sofa to turn on their own box. There wasn't much of a choice of programming—no more than for the rest of France, in fact, apart from a thrilling American drama from which no heart was immune, and today's was the last in the ten-episode series, which had by now acquired a serious following. Philippe was as interested as the two women in the romantic adventures of brilliant businessmen caught between catty, ambitious wives and degenerate children. Ludovic had seen one previous episode of the series and had fallen asleep almost instantly, to general disappointment. Still, he sat gamely on a sofa and stared at the little black box with a pretense at interest. After ten minutes of advertisements followed by opening credits scrolled over an introduction of beautifully tragic music, all became absorbed by the story.

Back in the dining room, Henri Cresson had caught up with his management's unionized opponents and was already yawning a little as he listened.

The American series ended well, thank goodness, for the whole of France had just been in tears over it. The emotional moments had both women red-eyed, but Philippe had held firm in expectation of his brother-in-law's reaction, which would have meant a fortnight's mockery had he wept. Adopting an unmoved expression, he winked at Ludovic, who had watched the whole episode with sweet obedience and returned to life only with the triumphant closing credits.

On Henri's screen, the two leaders were bidding each other goodbye and good riddance, having dropped all pretense at subtlety, with elections approaching and the politicians short on time to go into the whys and wherefores. The end of the two cronies' digressions caught him by surprise, so he went back to the realm of the humans he was used to frequenting despite himself for some time already.

"They spent the whole time talking nonsense. A pair of idiots! Our poor country!" he said, not without substantial self-satisfaction, for he'd made a tidy sum at the stock exchange the day before, though he'd only been able to toast it with his secretary, who had literally kissed his boots in celebration.

There wasn't even much call to inform his family. So he rose abruptly and went on.

"Anyway, it can't be said—or not without some dire self-delusion, for your own gastric rumblings were audible through all four salons—that their sparring disturbed your American claptrap!" Then he added, "Right. I wish you all good evening."

And, quite as abruptly, Henri straightened his suspenders, which had been lowered for relaxation; aimed a flying kick at a Khmer statuette that had strayed into his path, which described a brief flight into a Moroccan cushion; then disappeared, apparently for one last lap around the park.

The air did feel mild outdoors that autumn evening. Ludovic might have joined Henri had the other television watchers not wanted to share their emotional reactions, their pain or passion for the series' three heroes.

After sharing a number of sensitive and refined comments on the marvelous soap (only Americans are able to combine these kinds of "settlement" with their well-known technique), and after emphasizing the characters' generosity of spirit, their warmth and intelligence, Sandra had a go at repeating the show's final line: "Yes, my dear Mrs. Scott, you do love him, but not enough to die of it, for love can sometimes hurt us quite to death, and it only stops then." First expressed by the heroine's Black nanny, these words were now repeated in the accent of the healthy-looking "good" slaves that are often seen in such period films, an accent unexpected from the first lady of La Cressonnade. Her attempt at a jaunty Southern intonation sent her brother, Philippe, into an irremediable fit of giggles, which had him fleeing to his room. The two women went on, discussing how they personally would have behaved ("Yes, yes, we must admit it") in certain scenes. Seeing her stepson's feet poking out above a sofa—a Mexican one, perhaps, or Bedouin, they couldn't be sure—Sandra brought him into the discussion, with a touch of compassion.

"How about you, Ludovic, have you been in love?"

"I've hardly seen it all," he admitted, "but the dialogue that came at the beginning seemed a little . . . clunky, to me."

"We couldn't expect any better from him," said Marie-Laure, to her disappointed audience. "Ludovic hasn't seen five whole films in his entire life, nor, doubtless, has he read more than ten books. Nor admired more than a single painting."

Smiling and untroubled by the women's scornful tones, Ludovic calmly observed that he had always read and enjoyed poetry; then, confronted by their doubtful faces, he suddenly recited a couplet from the "Dancing Serpent," about eyes like iron-hard jewels.

"Even in poetry you show such bitterness about women," Marie-Laure said. "Poor Verlaine!"

"That was Baudelaire, I believe," he gently corrected her, only annoying her further.

Now more put out than triumphant, she laughingly told him, "Do check tomorrow in the dictionary."

Then she took the arm of her mother-in-law (herself quite incapable of telling the two poets' work apart), who, rather emotional and tired, clung to her as they climbed the stairs. Together they went up, stiff as two goats, Marie-Laure with her chin crossly pointing the way, for anger always enhanced her physical determination.

◆ ◆ ◆

Inside the drawing room, Martin, the butler, had already meticulously turned off the lamps and the television. The only light left in the room was the glaring illumination over the stairs. In the midst of all these widely disparate decorative eras, united in their authentic ugliness, this electrified aspect felt almost comforting. Henri Cresson required that bourgeois rules be observed in his house and had not personally touched a light switch for some time. Now and then he had Sandra's forty-watt bulbs replaced by two-hundred-watt ones; he found his wife's feeble illuminations depressing. He had even decreed that new bulbs could not be less than eighty watts anywhere in the house.

Sandra knew quite as well as Henri that leaving lights on, televisions flickering, or any similar foolishness could become a very expensive indulgence, but she nonetheless could not ascend a staircase in the dark, a hospital trip being more expensive than a light bulb. So she called out to Ludovic, still alone in the drawing room.

"Don't forget to turn the staircase lights out, will you!"

The last affectionate words of a loving stepmother.

◆ ◆ ◆

Ludovic and Marie-Laure's bedroom was the newlyweds' one or, on occasion, the injured newlyweds'. It was a large room on the far side of the house, looking out over hilly country and from which a little staircase went down to a kind of study with a chaise longue where the young couple could take naps or read a little between frolics.

Naturally, Ludovic, the miraculous revenant and ex-simpleton of the family, was supposed to spend his nights of passion with his wife, but the little camp bed, the plant, and the few books that furnished this ground-floor snug were much more to his taste for the time being.

This study's tall French windows to the terrace stood open. Ludovic stepped in through them, rapidly undressed, and pulled on a rather comical set of pajamas that would better have suited a baby—but he was used to them, he felt. He lit the two little side lamps and began climbing the steps that connected the two rooms.

"Marie-Laure? Marie-Laure?" he called softly.

His wife roughly banged the door open.

"What do you want?"

Her words echoed down the stairs and out through the open French windows and floated off from there, at which the murky shadow of scandal prompted her to lower her volume abruptly. She went on in a fluting little voice, hissing between her teeth and all the more aggressive.

"What do you want? What do you want now?"

"I'd have liked to join you," said Ludovic slowly, in tones of exquisite politeness. "I should have liked to be with you again."

"Never! I told you—never!"

Marie-Laure had come down a step and was now leaning over him, her apparently ageless face convulsed with rage and bitterness. Dressed in a long evening kimono from whose deep sleeves her thin hands and painted nails emerged and clutched desperately, as if trying not to slaughter him, at the two narrow rails on either side of the stair, she suddenly appeared, in a fascinating if frightening way, like one of those enormous bats you see that frighten children in zoos.

Ludovic drew himself back at once, and he, too, automatically grabbed the little wooden handrail. Thus they appeared less like two lovers absorbed in lovers' games and more like two mortal enemies wishing each other dead.

At least so they appeared to Henri Cresson, who was resting in the shadow of a plane tree and now had a direct view of his daughter-in-law's face as well as that of his sagging son. They were only ten meters away, so Henri watched and listened to all that spilled from that brightly lit French window: words and images that left his own face stony.

"I'm cured," Ludovic responded slowly. "I love you and I'm cured."

"Listen, I didn't mean to say it so roughly, but your persistence every evening gives me no choice: you're not cured and you never will be! I saw you every time we visited; I saw you in straitjackets, crawling, biting, drooling, laughing like a donkey with your idiot friends—how could I forget that? It was horrendous! Do you really think I could have a wild and vicious animal in my bed? I could never embrace you, you see; think about it . . . There's no woman alive who could. The empty eyes, the dangling arms—it's repugnant! Do you see? Don't you see at all?"

Henri, who from his post could see only his daughter-in-law's outraged face and Ludovic's slumped shoulders, now wore a strange expression: a furious, wood-hard mask, like they make for idols on distant islands.

"I've never been vicious," said Ludovic. "I was sedated."

"How would you know? Ludovic, we should divorce. As quickly as possible, please, after the party! Good night."

She turned and climbed back up her section of the staircase, tripped at the last step, and stumbled back into the bedroom, which stripped some of the drama from her exit.

Ludovic turned slowly too and descended the steps, then went to lie on his bed. His face bore the same expression as his father's: neutral and faraway, stony blank but without aggression. When he lit a cigarette with a dodgy old match, he did so without the least difficulty or wobble.

# 3.

The sparkling pale sunlight of Austerlitz, indeed of all Touraine that day, filled Ludovic's monastic bedroom and drew his sleep-softened features out of ease and back to sadness. He blinked and remembered the man who, he now knew, would always fill his wife with a sense of disgust and alienation. He dug his head back into the pillow with a miserable whimper. When he opened his eyes, instead of the vigorous arm he used to wield, he saw a teenager's bony wrist poking out of his eternally too-short pajama sleeve. With Marie-Laure's explanation, the loneliness, fear, and disappointment he'd been feeling since his return now felt even crueler than the bleak and endless days that had preceded this. He couldn't even blame the man he had both so rapidly and so slowly become, behind the sanatorium's thick glass doors, for the attitudes, the physical presence, and the repugnance he now knew he inspired. Ludovic had never cared enough about himself—he'd never had the time, in fact—to think about killing himself and so abbreviating a life he'd hardly had time to enjoy. There were no mirrors in the sanatoriums, only the merest square of glass for shaving in, and that only if the nurses could be convinced of your drive to live. So it had been two years before Ludovic saw himself again for the first time. When the ambulance carrying him back to La Cressonnade stopped outside a pharmacy, he had spotted the face of an odd and feverish tall young man reflected in its windows. On his reaching La Cressonnade, Sandra's and Marie-Laure's "How you've changed!" exclamations, without further details, had not sunk in at the time. On the other hand, Martin's satisfied expression—"Monsieur is looking so very much better than last time"—had made him laugh: naturally, for Martin had last seen him entirely comatose and already in receipt of extreme unction.

Somewhat uncharitably, Sandra had detected a whiff of fraudulence in that last sacrament, literally extorted by a cleric horrified at the thought of an atheist in eternal purgatory. At bottom, what she most regretted in her stepson was a kind of deviousness, although she did not mention this until later. She feared an ear-bashing from her husband who, though mostly respectful, at times gave way to indefensibly violent actions. For example, in the early days of their marriage, notionally to prompt her to be quiet, he would give her little taps on the shoulder that, when she went on chattering, would turn into veritable batterings, great slaps between the shoulder blades, which knocked her off balance. Or, alternatively, violent embraces that squashed the breath out of her, her husband squeezing her with a vigor that made her reconsider her plans to tell all about Ludovic and his latest hypocrisies. This time, Henri had crushed her to his chest like a jealous bear and whispered into her ear, "So would you rather he'd died?" which patently was not the case. But the cleverest men don't always have access to the finesse demanded by certain scruples. Though also a woman, Marie-Laure, too, had not understood her mother-in-law's views.

◆ ◆ ◆

It was early—very early for La Cressonnade's hosts, "but the master of the house departed at dawn," as Sandra told everyone who was already up and gathered in the dining room (she had been brave enough to come down) with her customary mix of admiration and commiseration.

"It's not enough that he leaves for the office at eight in the morning." She was working up a head of steam. "He was up and out at six! And when I asked him why, he gave me such an odd reply . . . I must have misunderstood."

Her little giggle of confusion was so flirtatious that it drew the gaze of everyone present.

"We could help you investigate," said Philippe. "We're all quite used to your husband's tricky ways."

"He did reply on paper: 'My dear little one, stay in your bed with the old feathers of your pillows and certainly don't think of budging before my return!'"

Philippe, Ludovic, and Marie-Laure burst out laughing. Sandra joined in, setting the stool she was perched on wildly wobbling; a structure created of mica and fabric, it was flameproof, stainless, unbreakable, and inoxidizable but also nonrefundable and, in short, execrable. Her only option was to drop gracefully onto the Moroccan pouf, which was better suited to her scale.

Sandra raised a finger to summon the butler, Martin.

"That should be sent back to that factory in Sweden or wherever it came from," she said, with a severity intended to add ballast to the statement.

"That factory went out of business sixty years ago," murmured Philippe. "I am sorry. Which reminds me: I was hoping to present you with a garden chair from the same designer—they were called Checker—but they are, alas, undiscoverable; in short: over."

"Beautiful and original things are no longer in fashion," his sister lamented, cutting herself a fresh slice of cake—her first slice having fallen beneath the "zebu," an inaccurately named animal whose skeleton, skin, and head had been preserved thanks to repairs as frequent as they were laborious.

What was more, this atrocious beast, unknown even to the most recherché museums, had horrified all the children and animals quite as much as it disgusted the adults. Over time, foolhardy dogs had bitten chunks out of it, its hair had fallen off along with its scales, and it no longer looked like anything so much as the biggest and ugliest animal on planet Earth since the time of the diplodocus. This zebu creature occupied pride of place in the drawing room, its enormous tail coiled around an imitation of Tutankhamun's sarcophagus and its head abutting the Gothic armor that had once belonged to a cleric of the Inquisition. In any event, this relic was not gentle on the eyes. But the family hardly noticed it these days; only newcomers were still frightened by it, for it must have been a giant among its kind (without, as Sandra liked to claim, being the snooty diplodocus's triumphant challenger).

◆ ◆ ◆

Sure enough, Henri had risen very early, after a bad night's sleep. Yesterday's bout of Marie-Laure versus Ludovic as observed from his plane-tree post had upset him. While not exactly his son's most attentive protector, he had nonetheless grown used to believing him happy; now he saw his son unable to be happy again. For a sinister and unequal struggle was unfolding under his own roof, in which the designated victim was Ludovic, his flesh and blood—and his responsibility. Henri awoke, then, in a bad mood, which turned into a rage directed at himself, at people, at the rest of the family, at everything that, bar total abandonment—definitive abandonment like his first wife's—could come between human beings and drive them to pair off and live together like miserable domestic pets.

Some would say that Henri was forever in a bad mood, or perpetually about to fly off the handle, but they would be wrong. He justified his temperament with reasoning that was entirely logical by his lights: a business deal that hadn't worked out, someone defying him, a pretty woman giving him grief, anything he wasn't keen on. In this case, at least, he had a role to play. But what exactly was it?

Ah yes: he must introduce that great clodhopper Ludovic to a well-established prostitute. So he stepped into his car, remembered that people generally parked very badly on that lady's street, then decided he would nonetheless find a spot. And he did.

Madame Hamel was there waiting for him, having arrived well before Henri, although he didn't know it. She'd had time to give the bar a little seeing to with the feather duster, and had selected two stools and arranged them at a little distance from the rest, as if these simple wooden objects for sitting on could become unwanted witnesses. She had also taken out a bottle of whisky, one of Ricard, one of Perrier, and one of Coca-Cola. You never knew: men changed, and the tastes of some tended to the ever more bizarre.

Henri stepped inside with a relaxed stride, crossed the little hallway as he would any familiar place, and, having reached Madame Hamel, clasped the tips of her fingers, bent, and kissed them. She adored that, he vaguely recalled. Doubtless it had something to do with her vision of how gentlemen behaved.

He sat on the stool beside her, let his hand hover over the four bottles, then got down again, landing on tiptoes, for—perhaps the reader is unaware—he was only of middling height and rather short in the legs. So he jumped down from his perch, went in search of a bottle of vodka, and brought it back to the bar, where he perched once more with another little effort and set his trophy down in triumph.

Unhappy at his serving himself, Madame Hamel scuttled around him with great fuss, looking for ice and soda, unless he would prefer Indian tonic water? Eventually she came to rest, poured herself a vodka too, and they toasted like old friends, or like people who knew each other no longer or not at all, which was closer to the truth.

"As lovely as ever," Henri said somewhat coldly; compliments bored him when he paid them and were even worse from others.

"You're teasing," she replied. "Ever the gentleman, but you are teasing me."

"Never over serious matters," he said, then smiled.

He downed a slug of vodka as, suddenly, his plan began to appear challenging, even absurd, or in any case far too attractive and appealing for this woman made up like a schoolmarm. For her part, Madame Hamel saw right away that the conversation would not be the easiest and tossed a few pleasantries his way—the very thing, she knew, for breaking a little surface ice. How was he doing? Why were they not seeing him around these days? Was he pleased with his latest deals? All everyone talked about was him and his successes . . . all over Paris, even, or so it appeared. Was he really considering a move into politics? Henri let this wash over him, with the exception of the last sally, which he answered with a simple sweep of one palm toward the floor.

"Politics—never! Hogwash, strictly hogwash!"

She nodded her assent.

"Right!" he said, clapping that palm to the bar. "I don't want to waste your time. My problem is this: You are aware that my son, my only one, Ludovic, had a very serious accident?"

"Yes, of course, of course I am."

"Good. You will know that afterward we allowed him to be dragged through various ridiculous so-called health clinics where he wasted his time, my money, and a good deal of his, err . . . his shrinks' lousy drugs. You are aware of all this? Of course. However hard we try to be the model of discretion."

He chuckled grimly. Strangely, Madame Hamel was put out. She had thought of everything except that he might want to talk about his son. It was quite odd.

"Indeed, we don't talk about your son enough! We do talk about him, of course, but only stupid speculations. No one knows anything, or not these days."

"Precisely," said Henri. "Have you seen him?"

"Of course not; he doesn't come into town. The town hall's gardener happened to bump into him when he was going to drop something off at the house, no idea what. He thought Ludovic looked well, from a distance, a bit thin—but they didn't speak. It isn't clever, this hiding away. Your Ludovic ought to get out more, show his face, show everyone that he isn't . . ."

She stopped and shrugged.

"That he isn't crazy?" Henri finished for her. "Well, he isn't, even supposing he ever was. On the contrary, he was brain-washed by some idiots. And he'll be back at work shortly, but all of this has thrown him for a loop, you understand? Two years of being stuffed with the full gamut of tranquilizers—that never helped anyone."

"Of course you're right," Madame Hamel said with a nod, ready to follow up with some instructive story of her own, which he brushed away before she could begin. So she went back to her attentive silence.

"He hasn't had a woman in two years. Like all of us Cressons, he has a—shall we say—a lively temperament, and he's been deprived of women for two years, which is very bad."

"But his wife went like a shot to join him and help look after him, didn't she? What a delightful daughter-in-law you have there, and she's gorgeous too, of course, and—"

He cut her short. "No: she may be pretty, but she's a hussy—a social climber, in fact, precisely not what my sweet, naïve, thoughtful boy needs in his life. He won't be growing out of that," he said, with a touch of nostalgia. "Well, be that as it may, she's telling him it's unthinkable for a woman to get back together with a man who's been mad. And she's freezing him out, so there you are. She's barring him from her bed."

Madame Hamel gave a great start, which almost had her on the floor. Those words, "barring him from her bed," made up the single most horrifying line to her ears.

"But this . . . this is demonic! And illegal, to boot, did you know? You can demand . . ."

Henri Cresson's face showed there was nothing to be demanded other than that she hear him out.

"What do you intend to do?"

"I intend to reassure him on this point as soon as I can. I'm sorry you haven't seen him. He has come back even better looking than before, and more charming. He was always a handsome boy, as you recall."

"Why yes, of course he was," she replied, nodding. "He was a gorgeous lighthearted boy, all the girls liked him, and what's more, they all fell for him too. Your son was a very fine young man and I fail to see how some medication could . . . could suck that out of him."

"Neither do I. What's required is one of your . . . young ladies to reassure him. Does this seem a reasonable project to you?"

"Naturally," Madame Hamel said, despite an instant prick of slight unease at the revelation of Ludovic Cresson's unhappy, strange, even worrying reputation.

And then the choice of young lady was no simple matter. Let's see: Who would do . . . who? Profiles and faces began to dance before her eyes. Too young, that one; too silly, this . . .

"Of course, we can't be dealing with some young bimbo, or one with hang-ups," Henri added, bluntly. "What we need is a woman, a good woman who truly likes young men and knows how to look after them in circumstances such as these. Are we agreed?"

"Wait, wait a moment . . . I have a charming young lady in mind, not one you're acquainted with yourself; she has just moved to Paris—to Clichy, rather—a bold little thing."

"My son doesn't want some female adventurer!" Henri rapped back, annoyed, and gave the bar another good thump. "All he needs is a fresh lease on life. I mean, we just need to give him a leg up. Soon as it's done, everything will be much better. For him and for us."

"It must be a dreadful situation—for your poor wife too."

"Pah, she has no idea. She never has ideas about anything, more's the pity. But *he* knows because his hussy of a wife told him, and he thinks he's become unattractive. Which is far from the case. Anyway, it's quite simple. I'll drive him over to see you after lunch."

"Now, now, Monsieur Cresson, you must be joking; I trust you implicitly! This strapping young man . . ."

He gave the bar yet another hefty slap.

"That's precisely why! I want you to see him. You'll either go accusing me of missing something crucial, or you'll be in perfect agreement with me. I shall be back around half past two."

That very instant he turned on his heels and left. Somewhat flushed and flustered by the delicacy of her commission, Madame Hamel took up paper and pen and began to note down names, which flowed onto the page like a spring tide.

It was half past twelve, maybe one o'clock. Henri could easily have gone home to lunch and returned with Ludovic in tow afterward, but he paused to think for a moment: already, dining with his family exhausted and irritated him and destroyed his mood; two meals with them in one day would be quite unbearable. So he stopped midway at an inn he knew, where he lunched on a delicious *andouillette*—his wife's aversion to this tripe sausage had barred it from her table. He still had to phone the house to stop Ludovic from vanishing into thin air after lunch and so being elsewhere when he eventually reached home.

His call was picked up by Martin in his "man of logic" voice, a sign that he must have committed some idiocy, in which case, his expression more impassive than ever, he would be looking rather like Spock, whom Henri and Ludovic adored. Mr. Spock was the only fictional character they had both first encountered and, moreover, appreciated, together.

"The ladies and gentlemen are . . ." the butler began in a cold and doleful tone.

"I'm not asking you where they are; I'm asking you to fetch one of them for me. That said, never mind. Could you just tell Ludovic that I'll come and pick him up after lunch?"

"Monsieur will come to collect monsieur after lunch? Very good. I shall tell him, monsieur."

"Are you all right, Martin?"

"Quite all right, monsieur, thank you."

Henri put the phone down hurriedly. There must, once again, have been some domestic drama at La Cressonnade, and he congratulated himself on the instinct that had spared him the brunt of it for at least an hour. "Comfortably settled in an English armchair with your dog at your feet, a good bottle of Scotch, and a good fire in the fireplace"—he seemed to hear such lines now and then: the daydreams of a work-shy imbecile.

To go back to Henri's early-morning wakening and his precipitate arrival at the factory, incidentally deserted at that hour: the malaise that had driven him there had not yet dissipated. The several oddities he had since committed—that is the word—had in no way distracted him. In point of fact, under his own roof and without his realizing it, there was a dark struggle taking place of which he knew nothing at all: first unpleasant point. Secondly, the balance of power was turning out to be entirely skewed: one of the two adversaries was delicate and the other was fierce; the former being the sweeter and more impressionable one, nothing could be done about the situation. And thirdly and finally, to cap it all, the victim was his own flesh and blood, the very closest kin—being his very own and only son.

Ludovic's character—such as Henri perceived him these days—this semi-eclipsed boy, vulnerable to everyone around him yet defendable by none, was protected only by his three-year-long silence. Of course, Ludovic himself had politely refused to see or hear the infuriating meanness, the beyond ridiculous and—to Henri's mind—grotesque attitude of Marie-Laure. After his discovery that the latter refused to go to bed with her husband, that it was now a month since she'd first refused, that Ludovic was putting up with her refusal, and that she was dragging his manhood through the mud, Henri saw things differently. For that made a great many evenings when she had said the very worst things to a man who loved women—and God knows Ludovic did love them, much more than Henri, for his love always entailed affection, protection, and delicacy. Perhaps Henri had seen the worst, yesterday evening under that providential plane tree, seeing those two faces from afar—one of them ravaged by shame, fear, and refusal to believe that matters couldn't still be mended—when he heard that bitch's appalling declaration. This was a bitch whose pretty little face, waved before his son, had turned murderous: that of a young woman who was ready for anything.

And Henri considered how some young people would crumble or retreat into cowardice before this species with which they were obliged to have children and build the rest of their lives. Certainly, Henri himself was afraid of no one, not even of the type of creature who would likely have appealed to him, and he was not unaware of his own natural fierceness, his instincts for survival, for pleasure and control, being even more inexorable than his drive for destruction. But he had now attended a rehearsal of what doubtless would be the final moments of a destiny that could have been, that indeed had been, happy—for Ludovic, he knew, was readier than most for happiness. But for now, it was as if his son had been struck by lightning: he seemed, at times, to have an almost angelic, even a ghostly look about him. Ludovic absolutely must regain his confidence, and that sweetly styled gorgon in her perfect twinsets, that wife so elegant of body and so vulgar of mind, that heartless woman absolutely had to bite the dust.

In his youth—aged maybe twenty—Henri Cresson had read all of Balzac, and in the showiest and busiest periods of his life, he had returned to that fictional world where man is often sentimental and, for Henri's taste, a little cowardly; to a world of desertions and emotional disasters peopled by victims and cads, by social-climbing nobodies and great wealthy idiots. Ah no, no! His Ludovic had nothing in common with those puerile cynics, nor with the pretentious creeps. A proper man did not use women to make his fortune. And if Henri put up with some of that in his poor brother-in-law, Philippe, it was solely because, as his wife's brother, the man had joined his family, was poor as a church mouse, and wore his poverty like a disease as awful and pitiful as shingles or polio.

Sitting at his desk, lost in these cogitations, Henri snapped three or four pencils and tore apart several notebook pages, out of which he fashioned paper darts to inform those on floors below, specifically his secretaries, that above all he must not be disturbed or gainsaid at any time that day. A dart launched from his upper-floor sanctuary and floating down to the polished tiles of the ground floor was understood as a bugle call to order for his entire staff.

Sylvia Hamel had been born in Tours sixty-eight years before. After ten years devoted to travel and to her education, she had returned with her fortune made or, in any case, having acquired the technique and the resources to supply her fancies. This was all the easier in a town where she was honorably acquainted and where the news of her good fortune, of her praiseworthy, even honorable work, and of her various successes while abroad had been able to filter through. This was one thing she had learned: never let people forget you or discredit you. Absence can easily discredit the most respectable among us; for country people, especially, in the eyes of whom not residing in your hometown implies you're debarred from living there or you no longer wish to live there, either case indicates at least a moment's weakness.

For ten years—that is, ever since her return—the round-faced, white-haired, somewhat portly, and altogether provincially elegant Madame Hamel, as proprietor of a private household where she occasionally put up unfortunate young women who'd been beaten by their husbands or assaulted by life, had held a surprising range of roles in the good city of Tours. She led a troupe of society women—well, women of the local society, but still opulent and alluring—who, suffering the odd bout of charity as one would an attack of smallpox or cholera, were to be seen all over town, upon the madam's instructions, visiting those in need. Thus, Madame Hamel kept up two not-unrelated roles in that she looked after men's bodies and women's minds. And had quite naturally taken over leadership of the town, the only conurbation that really mattered to her although she had lived in Lyon, Miami, Detroit, and, to crown them all, Orléans, the final stretch of her girdle round about the wide earth. Any marriages or other alliances she may have made during those ten years remained unknown, but it was known that she retained firm connections in certain influential circles and that anyone who dared to cause her annoyance would be committing a grave error.

Between the Saint-Eustache church, where she managed the choir, the accounts, and the priest—a poor man of thoroughly disturbed mind, her reasons for ardently defending whose cause remained obscure—and all the charities, not forgetting a few slightly illicit ones that she looked after, she never lacked for power. Always, in the face of vicissitudes and troubles, Sylvia Hamel trained her steely brow, her serenity, and her benevolent smile on the rich—and, now and then, when she was about to finish them off or buy them out, on the poor too.

Henri had long been a loyal client of the pretty escorts she was in the habit of sending him in descending order by aesthetic impact and technical mastery. Then his marriage to Sandra Lebaille had obliged him to end their rather too visible connection and to reroute his passions toward the capital and a few hotels located nicely midway. These places were where he found his charming girls next door nowadays. At least he always behaved courteously, politely, and efficiently, by his own lights.

◆ ◆ ◆

When Henri arrived back at La Cressonnade to collect Ludovic, his little family was lingering over dessert on the terrace. Henri was rather surprised to find this lunch tableau, with the backdrop of the park's finest trees and the scent of chocolate in the air, quite exquisite. From inside his car, he gazed at each member of the group. Sandra, a strong woman grown ridiculous; Philippe, her parasite of a brother and great dandy; and Marie-Laure, the joyless little bitch, sexless indeed as well as heartless. And the last of them on whom his gaze fell, and to whom he made a sign to join him, was by far the least dishonorable. A little odd, perhaps, a little drifty, too sensitive for his wife and certainly too innocent. Not that he, Henri, was any fan of innocence, which to his mind could only arise out of comedy or mental deficiency.

"Now where are you two off to?" Sandra called out just then.

Her annoyed squawk caught its two addressees off guard. Ludovic hurriedly slammed the car door behind him. Henri muttered a few inaudible things, then revved and made his escape, only slowing when they reached the little secondary road, these days relegated practically to a side road by a brand-new wide, triumphant highway that ran almost parallel and connected everything to everywhere, thanks to roundabouts as plentiful as they were pointless. Henri secretly preferred the good old road, which with its bonus ten kilometers avoided all roundabouts, all red lights and diversions—which skipped, in short, all the latest innovations.

Looking out on it from his passenger seat, Ludovic realized how bucolic but also how outdated this road now appeared. Cars no longer went this way. The distance markers looked like old milestones with their red-painted tops and weather-worn lettering. Left to grow wild, the green and yellow trees made benign, old-fashioned perils. It was the same story for the tin-backed advertising signs, most of them barely hanging on to their posts by a single metal strip and on which could be read, if you tipped your head sideways: "Land of Snails 300 meters," "Food and drink here," and "The Sign of the Jolly Joker," although not the slightest cheer could be detected above the silence of this landscape. In fact, this road had been defeated, outrun by the upstart rival whose hum could now and then be heard, a few kilometers away; this was a road to hide from children nurturing their faith in progress, speed, and anonymity. None of them would ever remember the Sign of the Jolly Joker for, like Henri Cresson, they would never set foot in the establishment.

Ludovic kept his own counsel. His father accelerated hard just at the point, after a bend, where they spotted some old-time cops, just three or four officers smoking and strolling in the other direction.

"Where are we going?" Ludovic began gently, in his most conciliatory, accepting tone.

*If I were to tell him we're off to plant peas in a village in Ecuador for three months, he'd say OK*, Henri thought. As few fathers are troubled by their child's powerlessness, he right away scorned his own apprehension.

"You remember Madame Hamel?" he asked, assuming an affirmative.

"Of course," Ludovic replied enthusiastically, then blushed, thus reassuring his father.

"I ran into her at my lunch place, and she has invited us for an apéritif at her house. She wants to show me her new herd—superior stock, it would seem. So I thought: *Now, how about Ludovic, still moping around La Cressonnade with nothing to do, since he still doesn't drive? Perhaps it would amuse him to* . . . Can't hold a candle to conjugal life, of course; we're in agreement on that point, I take it?"

Henri emitted a great guffaw, which was intended to be gravelly, conspiratorial, and intimate and which didn't suit him at all.

Madame Hamel was there, flanked by two gorgeous women who were made up as if for an evening out and seemed delighted to make their acquaintance.

The gradual disappearances, first of his father with one of the girls, then of Madame Hamel herself, left Ludovic and the other young woman alone in the small drawing room—which was actually done up rather like a dentist's waiting room, although veiled in almost nerve-rackingly low lighting. The hazy dimness led the lovely creature to huddle up close to our Cresson heir. The latter was shaking like a leaf, feeling the return of sensations so long barred to him that he now behaved more like a hussar than an experienced lover. Afterward Alma—for that was her name—asked whether he could come back the next day, but to her own place, where they would "be more comfortable."

He answered, "Yes, oh yes!" with an eagerness she found charming.

◆ ◆ ◆

Tickled by his own subtlety, Henri awaited his son outside the house and, as soon as Ludovic emerged, gave his sleeve a tug and couldn't resist also slapping his shoulder in congratulation, momentarily forgetting that Ludovic was all of thirty-something years old.

"We'll keep this off the record, of course?" he said. "If that harpy gets wind of this and starts spying on us . . ."

"I don't believe Marie-Laure even dreams of doubting my fidelity," Ludovic responded, thoughtfully but gaily.

"That's her mistake. Anyway, Caroline, Madame Hamel's latest protégée, was upset that you chose Alma over her. Let me tell you something, my boy: you have always been a fine specimen, but since your . . . your somewhat chaotic recent times, you've stepped up a class. You've acquired . . . err, how to put it . . . a new allure."

At this, like a pair of wary but swaggering young rogues, they exchanged secretive, almost triumphant smiles, such as they'd never before had the occasion or inclination to share.

On their way back to the house, Henri and Ludovic stopped at a roadside café called the Junction, where they shared a bottle of J&B. Then Henri stopped the car outside La Cressonnade's main gate and Ludovic got out there. He skipped his way back to the house with such a spring in his step that he looked like a happy simpleton, now and then hugging small trees in his path and vaulting the gates to the lawn like so many fences at a racecourse. Then he disappeared into his room, where he gave his reflection a smile of complicity which, had he been the type, he might have described as lascivious.

# 4.

The Paris train came into Tours station at 4:10 p.m., the scheduled hour. For the last twenty minutes, two starched and bow-tied men had been waiting on the platform, the younger of them fielding an empty luggage trolley. Henri Cresson, who detested waiting to an almost pathological degree, had already paced the length of the platform more than ten times, his son serving as a waymark as he passed him in each direction.

Only a very tenuous notion of respectability held Henri back inside that station. He was reflecting that Fanny might take on the required role, but then, too, that he was not sure of his choice. The only time they had met, at their children's wedding, the encounter had been ill-fated. The nuptials had been held four months after Quentin Crawley's death, and Fanny had been unable to present any public face, any features or expression beside the features, the expression, of grief. The extremely modest ceremony had been held in Paris, and Henri recalled it as a slow and boring nightmare. Only Ludovic's happiness had lent a bright note, some justification for those grim hours.

When the train came in and halted, now somewhat ahead of his son, Henri turned to the first-class carriages. There he saw a woman, the embodiment of elegance, descend the steps and, without a glance his way, smile upon the poor devil who was lugging her cases and practically thanking her for the privilege. There were two first-class carriages, of which Fanny's was at the front. The cress tycoon, the magnate of dried fruit and other foodstuff and nonsense, began to trot toward that fabulous form who, having adjusted her hat to a Garbo-ish angle, was enthusiastically shaking the hand of her anonymous porter, an unlucky fellow traveler who laid what might have been the tenth suitcase at Fanny's feet before jumping back into the departing train. No matter: she waved him off, and it was only after the train's disappearance into the distance that she straightened her hat once more, removed her sunglasses, and swept the platform with her luminous brown eyes, narrowed above a fine mouth with a ready, dazzling, and affable smile. An almost happy face, Henri thought, hastening toward her in spite of himself.

Renowned as one of the great fashion designer Kempt's most brilliant assistants, Fanny was also well known for her charm, courage, and warmth. She had a real lust for life—at least she had once, before her husband's death. Now she was doing an excellent job of pretending, no longer spending all her time trying to forget, even if it was sometimes a hard task.

Henri appeared before her and took her hand with both enthusiasm and consideration, the latter sentiment a rare one for him.

"Henri Cresson," he said, bowing.

"And I am Fanny Crawley. Excuse me: I hardly recognized you."

"Same here," replied Henri, with feeling. And he added, smoothly, "You were already very beautiful, but you were so very sad . . ."

As he shook his head, the very model of an emotional pro, Fanny Crawley's mocking chestnut eyes grew brighter and gentler. She laid a hand on his cheek, for an instant, and they both remembered walking down the bleak corridor of the hotel that hosted that wedding breakfast, and the equally depressing rooms in town. Both shook it from their thoughts as one, as if emerging from a drama instantly forgotten.

"Didn't we used to have married children in common, once upon a time? Where can they have gone?" Fanny inquired, laughing.

Which prompted Henri to remember what he was, in fact, doing on the platform with this stranger—such a beautiful stranger.

"Ludovic!" he cried.

He spun around and discovered his ninny of a son pinned down by the luggage trolley, which, being stuck, could go neither forward nor backward an inch. Strung like a bow against the confounded contraption, the young man was swearing softly but distinctly.

"What an idiot! I'll show him. Please wait here."

Fanny watched Henri march at a clip toward his son; square his shoulders; pull out a tiny, invisible but crucial valve; and roll the thing back to gain a bit of leverage. Unfortunately, the trolley responded to this new pressure by leaping suddenly forward and falling onto the tracks. Ludovic grabbed his father in midflight, who clung onto him in turn, which sequence set the pair dancing a rapid, ridiculous, but lifesaving jig. Each landed on his feet, stunned and panting. A delighted laugh restored their good humor.

"My God!" Fanny exclaimed. "Goodness, you frightened me! Are you Ludovic, then? I can hardly believe it. You were quite the playboy type when I saw you last; there was none of this studious look. You've grown thinner, I think."

Henri stepped in, shaking his head. "He has lost a good ten kilos, yes."

"Better to lose ten than gain them," she said. "Those damned tranquilizers will turn anyone old and fat in no time. But for you they do the opposite . . . Would you be good enough to bring one of these crazy trolleys for my cases?"

At his father's reproachful look, Ludovic mimed apology for his absentmindedness and set off to the far end of the platform at a canter.

"Don't worry," Fanny said to Henri. "I always travel with stacks of suitcases high enough to alarm my hosts but almost never open more than one of them."

Ludovic had vanished altogether, and Henri was losing patience.

"Now where has he gone? And you must be exhausted, what's more . . . What an idiot that boy is!"

"Well, don't forget that I am here specifically to remind all of Touraine that your son is precisely not an idiot."

Just then a triumphant Ludovic reappeared, back in view but at quite the opposite end of where they were expecting him and clearly now the absolute master of his machine. He halted before them and began piling the luggage onto the trolley— suitcases, trunks, and hatboxes, all as best he could.

"Such a lot of luggage!" he exclaimed.

Henri was writhing at this rudeness when Ludovic added, "How nice! It shows you're planning to stay a little longer with us."

And Cresson the younger turned to Fanny with a face so absurdly youthful, with such lonely eyes, with a mouth so ready to smile and a lower lip so full and generous that it alone spoke of sweetness, that Fanny thought, *He is so different and so much nicer than the son-in-law I had before.*

She watched Ludovic heap some of the luggage into his father's convertible—the rest would be delivered—then straighten his hat once more. Henri opened the front passenger door for her and she sat, showing her legs, naturally, over which Henri could not help casting the rapid, appreciative glance of a practiced seducer.

◆ ◆ ◆

Ludovic slipped in behind and settled crosswise on the edge of the back seat, between two rather hard suitcases and a hatbox overflowing with tissue paper.

"Won't you be driving, Ludovic?" she said suddenly.

And the actual driver stalled. Henri started up again but said nothing until they'd done a good two hundred meters.

"You know, Ludovic hasn't driven since the accident."

"But he wasn't the one at the wheel." Fanny's expression was severe.

"You are truly the only person who remembers that," Ludovic spoke up, his voice choked.

Then, thrusting his head suddenly between the two front seats, he laid his cheek on his mother-in-law's shoulder and sleeve. Even Henri was moved, for half a second.

But his two passengers might have preferred him to keep his eye on challenges ahead. For, as ever, Henri seemed to consider roads as so many avenues created for his personal use. He was astonished when another car dared to share one with him, only appreciating its paintwork, eventually, via his rearview mirror. Even Fanny, despite seeming remarkably absent-minded, could be seen directing worried glances at the downcast Ludovic, who refused to meet her eye until, unable to hold back any longer, he looked up and smiled at her, the way children smile when they're about to burst into giggles in class.

"Goodness, my dear Henri, why must you go so fast?" his visitor asked. "The countryside here is beautiful, striking, even."

"Bah," said the master of the house, accelerating. "Bah . . . You'll see; the house itself is still more striking."

"Oh. Besides, it hardly matters," she said, closing her eyes.

Fanny let her head sink back into the cushion.

From his awkward position, Ludovic examined the curve of Fanny's neck; her elegant, serene, patient, handsome head: it was one of those forms that travelers occasionally fleetingly encounter between one train and the next and that they remember all their lives, like a homesickness.

"Only three kilometers to go," the young man spoke up, in a melancholy voice. "I wish I knew you better."

"I would like to know you better too, my dear son-in-law," Fanny replied, and laughed. "I've seen you only three times, I believe: when Marie-Laure introduced you, when you married her, and, once, in one of those horrible places they put you for treatment after the accident."

"I remember that clearly," Henri said, abruptly. "You even burst out sobbing directly after. And as you were the only one to do so in three months, that stood out for me."

There was a silence.

"I remember . . ." Fanny's voice murmured, her eyes still closed, her face as calm as ever. "I remember that he was wearing . . . that you were wearing—excuse me, Ludovic—white twill pajamas, you were lying in a garden chair, asleep, and your wrists and ankles were strapped down although no one could have looked gentler than you. And I confess I did weep, yes. Not so much about you, though; I was thinking, I was sure you would recover, yes, that you would be out of there very soon. I wept about all those who were not weeping."

"But . . . but men don't weep," Henri retorted, in childish self-defense.

A very, very long silence fell, then, and lasted all the way to La Cressonnade.

When she emerged from the car, which Henri drew up with an elegant curving sweep, Fanny had recovered her gay and easygoing mood.

# 5.

Fanny had just time to see, like a nightmare, the medievalesque turrets erected by one of the widowed sisters-in-law before her departure and the machicolations along the house's opposite wing before Martin appeared on the perron, opened the visitor's door for her, and was releasing the herd of luggage crammed into the trunk (hemmed in by hats, Ludovic was left to fend for himself). Henri strode around the car and took Fanny's arm in order to lead her into his domain, while a triumphant Philippe, tumbling down the five steps to meet them—slicked-back, bow-tied, and ironed from head to toe, smoothing a pocket handkerchief that was very slightly too visible—was stunned to find two men at La Cressonnade, or three including Martin, who, as he rarely went outside its walls, was absurdly but also irremediably pallid. Philippe was struck by Martin's pallor, by the chalky hue he'd not noticed before and that he would have identified as a jailbird's color had he ever known people of that sort.

"Fanny, madame," Philippe said, stopping at the tenth step, where the parade made up of Henri, Ludovic, and Martin, the latter two staggering beneath the luggage, had come to a halt. "Fanny—may I call you Fanny? We have met twice, first at your daughter's wedding and secondly at Ludovic's bedside."

"I see you suffer from a selective memory," Henri groaned, "having chosen the decade's two most miserable moments."

The master of the house came to an abrupt stop on the landing as he said this, while behind him the line of people wobbled. Fanny had time to make a graceful though desperate leap down to the next landing, while Ludovic and Martin clung to the staircase and Fanny's precious cases flew in all directions.

"My clothes will be fine," she said to Henri. "Does Ludwig the Second's castle in Bavaria rise higher than yours? Do you have more than two hundred and seventy steps?"

Undaunted, Henri pointed to the right-hand corridor with a gallant flourish.

"Your daughter resides there," he said. "Ludovic will show you."

"I would feel it more courteous to greet your wife first."

"My sister is tired just now, but I suppose you will want to see your daughter," Philippe interjected. "It's only a little further . . . I mean your daughter and Ludovic's room, of course."

"It makes no difference," Ludovic said, avoiding the question. "The main thing is that Fanny should feel at home."

And he laughed as he followed the new detachment, leading their guest all the way to Marie-Laure. Walking ahead of everyone like a phantom tour guide, Ludovic stopped just before the last bend in the corridor.

◆  ◆  ◆

Fanny had agreed to this trip, the house, and the visit to her daughter so she could discover how married life was suiting the latter and also convey her appreciation of her son-in-law, a somewhat absurd mission and very out of character for her except, perhaps, given the rather tyrannical delusions she was diagnosing in Henri and the more desperate disconnection she could see in Ludovic. This was a mission she could only conceive as an unforeseen duty. After all, these two had no one else to impress now—half the time that's all men are doing. There was something larger than life about these comical upper-crust people, something so outside time, so out of step with the era and its ethos, that she felt a twinge of fear. These were wealthy people of whom one had married her daughter. Now his family wanted to rehabilitate him, yet they were the root cause for the state he was in, namely deep unhappiness. It had been a long time since Fanny had found anyone so primed with unhappiness as this boy; plainly, he encountered nothing but brick walls and silences in this house. This might even be worse than a Mauriac novel or books of that kind in which monsters confront each other, for there was no one monstrous here, except perhaps her daughter—but Fanny preferred not to think about that.

After a number of twists and turns and a distance about the extent of all twenty-four hours of Le Mans, or so Fanny felt, they stopped outside a grand door, recently repainted in a style that might correspond, among the Cressons, to a newly-weds' palette. It would be repainted for the children's weddings, those of the grandchildren, et cetera. No one dared to knock. Annoyed by the feebleness of his company, Henri lifted a fist and gave the door a great thump.

"Marie-Laure," he called in a voice he meant to be cheery but that came out rather threatening. "Marie-Laure, your mother is here!"

He was answered by an ungrateful silence. Fanny, beside him, saw the fine veins swell and begin to throb at his chin and temple. Henri knocked again, and now his voice had lost its last remnant of sugar.

"Marie-Laure! Christ! Are you dead? It's your mother, I tell you!"

He rattled the door handle in vain: it was locked. At this there was a genuine silence, one of those you characterize as sliceable by a knife, and certainly all present were frozen to the spot. Henri turned a rage-convulsed face to his son.

"So, your wife locks herself in, now? How do you go about reentering your room in the evening? Do you offer up prayers outside the door?"

Ludovic, ashen-faced, remained strangely firm in his silence and his lack of visible anger. Fanny stepped in between them and took her turn calling to her daughter:

"Darling . . . It's me, your mother . . . You were sleeping, I suppose. I'll expect you in my room in half an hour or so. That will give me time to take a shower. See you soon, sweetie."

And after a small, affectionate wave at the closed door, a gesture as useless as those that preceded it, she turned around with a firm step and, taking the still-crimson Henri by the arm and her still-lily-white son-in-law by his, Fanny walked everyone all the way back.

"I don't understand," Henri muttered, sending furious, meaningful looks in Ludovic's direction.

Behind them, Philippe—who, during such an incident, would dig his kerchief even more deeply into his pocket as if into a place of safety—was walking with a slight stoop, unintentionally adopting the very particular gait of one Groucho Marx.

71

"Here is your room, dear Fanny, the one reserved for our most precious guests. If you don't like it there are three others available to you. From today, it is you who decides everything in this house; please don't forget that."

"I have never had any sense of authority," she said with a smile, "and this room is delightful."

◆　◆　◆

The room was decorated with a slightly old-fashioned wallpaper, in a mixture of pinks and lilacs whose shades now seemed to merge together. Tall windows looked out over the terrace. A plane-tree bough was brushing against the glass; when Fanny went to open the window, a leaf tickled her cheek, as if in welcome. She smiled at the terrace, at that leaf, and at the silence all around her, savored it for perhaps the first time in her life. Fanny smiled and did not turn to share her pleasure with the shadow—the shadow that always stood just behind her.

There are so many stages to mourning. From the cruelty, the daily banality that at first leaves you numb, then later aware and resigned to the indifference—here known as "discretion"—of your dear friends as much as of your distant acquaintances; to everything that leaves you at a loss, almost bored, but that little by little draws you back into life and is not part of your mourning: the unfolding and changing days, the moments that now pass without him, without her, without the two of you. And it isn't the certainty of another being, another story and another happiness to come that keeps you alive, but simply, perhaps, *le dur désir de durer*—"the hard desire to endure"—that the poet Eluard describes and that is born with you, between your mother's legs, that keeps you alive. In that moment, it is mourning for yourself that must be borne, a contempt without memories, even for the happy days. It's this unending black contempt for yourself, this machine of pain, which at night turns you back into an animal, whimpering beneath the sheets, and by day, an anonymous face holding back tears. You resist, you fight, and despair helps as a façade and a banality. A vague respect surrounds the leaky puppet you have become and makes you respectable, occasionally even attractive to others. But if that other is genuinely interested in you, in your pain and refusal; if your refusal is not too humiliating; if that other knows that a beaten heart is still a beating heart, then it may all become once more a window open onto a terrace on a lovely autumn afternoon. And then the first leaf to fall upon your cheek is not a punch out of the past but an unimaginable joy, at once irrefutable and incomprehensible, a joy no matter what you call it.

As she put away her four blouses, her two sweaters, and her other hopelessly well-cut clothes in the wardrobes of her deliciously old-fashioned rooms—with a vast and ancient bathtub in the bathroom—Fanny savored every instant of this peace, the only noise she could hear being the parquet's slight crackling beneath her feet.

◆ ◆ ◆

Ten minutes later, Marie-Laure knocked and stepped inside, finding Fanny with her back to her, hooking up her clothes hangers. So it was in her mirror that the mother examined her daughter from toe to top (fully five centimeters shorter than her mother, Marie-Laure had always found their height difference inexcusable).

Marie-Laure was wearing a gorgeous dress of pale mauve cotton and a very pretty piece of dark malachite jewelry at her neck that set off her eyes remarkably. She wore woven rope sandals that made her look more like a teenager than a young woman. For a moment Fanny thought she saw three people in the mirror, a notion she'd had ever since she could remember, which may indicate the absence of truth or humanity in all typical relationships.

Turning abruptly, Fanny gave her daughter a look filled with nostalgia for a long-lost childhood. After those three seconds of presiding over all their encounters and stage entrances, Marie-Laure closed the door behind her and ran the five steps to her mother. Fanny rested a hand on the rail of hangers and lightly kissed her daughter's forehead before stepping back.

"Maman, I must apologize. I had such a sudden urge to sleep . . . and I had so wanted to be there waiting for you on the perron, yet I simply collapsed on my bed . . . and on top of that I was woken by the Gestapo!"

"Your father-in-law is a little highly strung, but your husband behaved beautifully," said Fanny firmly. "Since when do you put locks on your doors? And you are looking beautiful these days, my darling."

"That's a miracle," Marie-Laure replied slowly. "How long have I been here? How long has Ludovic been officially well and fit to lead his own life?" To her mother's surprise, she burst out laughing. "Do you realize, after three years of questions and prognoses, there hasn't even been a proper diagnosis?"

Fanny sat down on her huge bed. "So what are you doing here? Do you love him or don't you? Don't tell me this is all pure devotion . . . Divorce him, if you believe he is mad. You are sharing a bedroom. What is it you want, exactly?"

"I am no longer a wife, Maman. There are limits to my indulgence. And there are some things I cannot say, even to my mother."

*Especially to your mother*, Fanny thought, without hesitation or sorrow, so long had it been since she had let go of Marie-Laure and her own maternal feelings. She rose and went to the window, thereby avoiding the bed, the brightly papered walls, and the door, all the symbols of a life shared with another. Mother and daughter were not, however, without a degree of admiration for each other: Fanny for Marie-Laure's heartlessness, as one may look on someone made differently, neutered at birth; Marie-Laure for Fanny's warm heart, her affection, and her kindness—qualities, she thought, that could be deepened by working at them, like politics, which, along with some other disciplines, was well regarded and perfectly pointless for any career, but she'd never had the time or the inclination to try any of them.

"What a lovely terrace," Fanny said distantly, as she gazed out the window.

Marie-Laure joined her cautiously, breathing in the evening air and her mother's scent, suddenly wafted back to her from a childhood she hadn't loved, and even while it confirmed the aloofness that governed her life, that scent still pricked her with a gentle melancholy of her own. Even Quentin Crawley had been too masculine and perhaps too fearful to involve himself in the cruel and perfumed denials that make up some women's teenage years. *Where is my mother going,* she thought, *with her work as our lady of fashion? There's no future in it. No partner either!* Even though, for Marie-Laure, that last idea had no connection with love or romance.

*And where is she heading, at this Teflon age?* wondered Fanny, for her part, feeling a momentary responsibility for this woman born to thrive on and to embellish wasted time.

A cheery voice interrupted, calling them both—it was Ludovic, who was stomping around impatiently on the terrace like a schoolboy.

◆　◆　◆

Ludovic had no appointments that day. "Busy yourself around the house," his father had muttered to him. Henri had been fearing the arrival of some kind of sad old widow, hardly a symbol of "gay Paris"; all the scenes of that ill-fated wedding haunted him still. He had, then, no help from memory or desire, only a flat mental picture showing Ludovic walking beside a widow, showing her the different views of the terrace and the drawing room while Marie-Laure trailed behind them. However, everything had changed with Fanny's arrival. Now he was picturing her laughing in the shade of the great driveway while his son chuckled alongside. Perhaps a week from now he would find them just like this, only with Marie-Laure definitively out of the picture: an infuriating vision. Fanny Crawley with his son, in his estate or his drawing room, was a suggestive image, such as desire can provoke and such as jealousy may reinforce, even when there's not the slightest truth in it.

So it was Henri who provided the soundtrack to those September weeks. Sometimes it is those playing *e contrario* roles who unleash the most violent passions in their companions, caught despite themselves in uncontrollable contortions. Henri, who was hard-nosed, possessive, and pitiless in a thousand ways, had never been overcome by his own feelings, except with the pain and emptiness of his wife's death. Now, all of a sudden, he became jealous, subconsciously, and could do nothing to avoid it.

Since Fanny's arrival, the task of helping her naturally fell to Ludovic. After all, it was the declaration of his mental fitness that occasioned their soirée and his natural absentmindedness that led to their profligate spending on it: petits-fours and principal dishes, large and medium-sized starters, and pyramids of cream-filled profiteroles were on the menu; also, raking all the pathways and trimming all the park's foliage; not forgetting a provision of temporary staff almost tenfold the usual (thieving and incompetent as they were, by Martin's report). All this was the product, the price, and, ultimately, the responsibility of Fanny. Ludovic had, then, to show his mother-in-law the true sights: the various salons where she was to receive and so rehabilitate a series of wealthy characters, already thereby disagreeable in Fanny's eyes. The mission was challenging, but much less of a problem for Ludovic—whose natural ease and perfect indifference to society allowed him to cruise above it, or in any case to let it flow past him—than for Fanny, whose horror at these gatherings and her inability to inject the remotest sense of elegance into her surroundings was growing by the minute. All of this made her task quite as ridiculous as her own objective. What was she doing, without the man she had loved, with a daughter she didn't love, attempting to prove the recovery of a young stranger, or almost-stranger, whom she was finding better company this year than before but still quite strange? There had been, in her life, one or two periods of ease, of logical progress, of readiness for anything—well, for anything wished, hoped, and expected by those around her and grounded in a feeling, or feelings, even if merely ambition, that brought couples, souls, lovers, and parents together. Here there was nothing. Just short-sighted people struggling to admit to the monstrousness they were claiming to have put behind them.

In fact, if there were people who appreciated others intelligently, people who felt a real duty of affection and a right to some blinkeredness, at least they showed evidence of a little soul in their lives. The pretentiousness, indifference, and mild aggression in response to stupidity at La Cressonnade was founded on a complete lack of interest in anyone else. The gaiety Fanny had felt at the station and on her journey had evaporated. There was nothing left besides this huge, fat house full of staircases, machicolations, and self-centered people. Fanny had met and appreciated in their turn rich people, snobs, and the buyers her designer worked with, but she had never identified or met people as strange to her as these. It wasn't money that ruled here, nor ambition nor the taste for

79

power—nothing she had encountered before, but rather a kind of deliberate noncommunication practiced by the whole family, which chilled her to the core. There was never, she sensed, any real conversation between Marie-Laure and her mother-in-law, between wife and husband, between father and son. Each maintained his or her property and place in the hierarchy; no one was really interested in anyone else, even slightly. It all floated in the air amid the country breezes that only now and then succeeded in dispersing it.

# 6.

Fanny had decided that the sun would shine on the great soirée. The mere vision of two hundred strangers stumbling among the Moroccan poufs and the marble exclamation marks in the main salons would normally have made her flee right away. Being one of those people who like to take their chances and accept the outcome, she thought that if it poured that evening, she would stay inside with the demoralized guests and watch with them as the canvas structures, buffets, and tables she had ordered were washed slowly away down the terrace—no matter if, right behind her, the Venus de Milo would be enjoying the same view, over the heads of the last dripping guests. Who could then claim, given storms and in such an interior, that Ludovic Cresson was any madder than the others? Mission accomplished, then, should the weather be temperamental, but it would be slight consolation for Fanny, who was quite as bored by disaster films as she was by the antics of decorators, however famous.

◆　◆　◆

"But of course you may have free rein," Henri had declared on the evening of her arrival. From Martin's astonishment as much as from the other diners' sudden silence, Fanny understood that this was no ordinary concession among the Cressons, certainly not from the master of the house, who, to point to the grandeur of his statement, had addressed her with the corroboration of his "man of the world" smile, which actually made him look quite vulgar. With his bull-like physique and his notions of human relationships and his own importance, he could have been vulgar without the smile but, bizarrely, his vulgarity showed only when he was subconsciously trying to hide it.

In Tours, among the passions widely prompted by the talk rippling out of La Cressonnade, this "free rein" had made some waves, at least among the shopkeepers. The second event (likely to put a stop to all further quibbling over his mental health) was the message handwritten by Ludovic on childish notepaper inviting Madame Hamel to meet him at their forest cabin the following week. At first she was astounded, then flattered, and then furious. What was this? She had her house and her girls! She wasn't about to go gallivanting with the crazy son of an ex-client in some chalet! To think that she could offer all the prettiest girls in Touraine and that this little libertine was after a woman—herself!—on the wrong side of sixty! But these dramatic breast-beatings finally gave way to the card that trumps all others: curiosity.

At three o'clock on Saturday, Ludovic and Madame Hamel were standing face-to-face in the chalet of love, he in corduroy, she in a black suit and full armor of lace and braiding. By the end of a dialogue we cannot retell in its entirety, it became clear that Ludovic's intentions were pure but that he knew of his debt to the madam: it was thanks to her that he had rediscovered the joys of love and so been saved from a long depression. Then, apologizing for his postman-like role, he presented Madame Hamel with an envelope containing a more than generous sum that (she was not to know) originated with the sale of four of his watches, of which a gold one dated from his communion. Ludovic accompanied her back to her taxi, and she clasped him to her breast, eyes swimming.

Oddly, Sylvia Hamel spoke of this meeting to no one, despite having commented upon it liberally beforehand, and allowed the most romantic speculations to do the rounds. And she got into the habit of declaring: "Ludovic Cresson may be mad, but he's a gentleman." As for Ludovic, feeling rather a Casanova, he raced back to La Cressonnade as he always did but this time with a notch more enthusiasm. He wasn't merely rejoining a cold and taciturn stepfamily and his own hostile wife but also rejoining Fanny, that lovely, intelligent woman who would address him like a man.

# 7.

It was half past four that particular Saturday when, returning from his rendezvous with Madame Hamel at the forest pavilion, Ludovic paused on the terrace. Henri's car was gone. Such silence and solitude lay over the afternoon and the house that he stayed rooted to the spot for a moment. And then the music made him go on. It was emanating from the old study beside the drawing room, from the ancient Bechstein abandoned in that adjacent room, which was officially allocated to smokers, artists, and other abstract conversations; that is, for the last twenty years it had lain lifeless and empty. In fact, it had been so ever since Ludovic's birth, for he had neither seen the piano open nor heard a single note from it. He was enjoying this music until one phrase, one whole melodic line, unfolded and split his heart in two. *For once*, he thought to himself. He arrived, strangely out of breath, at the wall, close to the window from which this honey and poison were issuing, and there he saw Fanny's silhouette, far, far away, or so she seemed to him just then. As she returned to this heartbreaking theme over and over again, he felt a sensation of utter despair: he had never been sure of anything, never had anything; he had always been denied, frustrated by everything, by what was in this music, by what hung in the air too, surely, around him, by what must have been drifting around him in Paris, hovering everywhere he'd managed only to drag his lack of life, he who had never been able to see, to own anything. He leaned against the wall for a moment, eyes closed, and held back his tears. *Tears: pure extravagance in an adult*, he thought.

Wiping his eyes on his sleeve, he wondered, for the first time in a good while, what was happening to him. During those long periods when all possible medications were tried on him, Ludovic had been saved by his lack of interest in himself, by his absolute lack of esteem—or indeed of contempt—for himself. Denied any responsibilities except for the few dubious and sentimental ones he had occasionally invented, he seemed now to have no rights, having never had any before besides that of spending his father's money with ease and generosity. He had been a carefree and steadfast man, quite ignorant of his own happiness, who was then ripped from the flow of his easygoing life and was now a troubled man, a man resigned to his solitude by the years of despair that had passed over him. Deprived of affection since childhood, he had long felt like the invalid he had officially become.

◆  ◆  ◆

The music stopped; the window opened.

"Ludovic? What are you doing there? I thought you were . . . I don't know . . . playing tennis," Fanny stammered.

She had heard, from Philippe of course, about the boy's afternoon escapades, how he liked to let off steam. Till now she had paid little attention and had even tried to ignore it. But now, finding the young man distraught in front of her, apparently just emerged from some purgatory more than any kind of pleasure, she was worried.

"You're as white as a sheet; come here," she said, motioning for him to climb in through the window.

He did so, but so slowly that she made him sit squarely on the three-seater piano bench before settling herself there again. She looked at him curiously. Ludovic's serenity seemed unmovable, just like his tanned skin, suddenly now translucent, and his ordinarily distracted gaze, which today gleamed brightly.

She began again to pick out that melody, a few notes at a time, with her right hand. "What upset you?"

"I haven't seen that piano open since I was a child," he said. He waved his hand vaguely, indicating his rapture.

"You've never seen anyone play it? That's unbelievable! It's a very good Bechstein, underplayed but the sound is very good. I did ask Martin if he could find a tuner. The one he found came this morning and turned out to be very discreet. The walls here are so thick. God—and so ugly!" she couldn't help adding, despite her self-imposed ban on critiquing the Cressons' interior decoration.

"What is it? That melody made my heart miss a beat," he said—and blushed. "You know, I'm quite ignorant about music. In the clinics I managed to buy a super little transistor radio, with little earphones, which meant they would leave me in peace sometimes. It's crazy what I listened to," he said, without the slightest annoyance at the music inflicted on him then in radiophonic slabs.

He could equally have said, "I was dying of boredom but then, just because I was demanding they come up with a diagnosis, those bastard doctors put me away for even longer; then they left me locked up, accused me of chronic feeble-mindedness and made me out to be an ongoing danger. Worst of all, no one defended or protected or tried to get me out of there, neither my own father nor my wife. Because they took everything from me, even my confidence as someone who knew how to live. Because ever since, I've been an object of humiliation. Because I visit whores now and then, to break up my loneliness."

Freshly determined, Fanny tore her eyes from his and went back to her theme on the piano.

"It's by Schumann," she said, her voice shaking slightly. "A quartet, I think. Very, very lovely, I agree. And it does go straight to the heart, you're right. I don't really play; I hardly know how, you know . . . There are some composers I like . . ."

They were sitting between the piano and the window. A playful, ironic sunlight was working its way through the shutters, shining in Ludovic's glossy hair and Fanny's wide eyes, which she kept fixed on her right hand and on the exquisite, aching honey of Schumann.

"I discovered this music here, today," Ludovic announced, abruptly. "And that makes sense because this is the first time that I have felt love, that I feel able to love someone. It's you I love," he said. "And now I can't live without you."

"Now . . . you can't be serious . . ." Fanny stammered, attempting to laugh and draw away from him along the piano bench.

But she only managed to tilt back her head, which, with Ludovic's mouth in hot pursuit, was soon captured. He was leaning with both hands on the piano bench while his lips alone nestled and were pressed to her cheeks, her forehead, and her neck, respectfully, irresistibly, with an ecstatic gentleness that had her whimpering in his sway. And these words went on ringing in the air: "I love you, I love you," spoken at last in a voice of complete assurance. Nothing enabled Fanny to push him away, for he wasn't holding her, wasn't touching her; there was only his mouth moving here and there, that most natural of things, that marvelous serenity, and the surging beat of their blood.

Dusk was falling but they paid no attention. Ludovic was babbling passionate nonsense, and astonishment, gratitude, and possessiveness were already mingling with all the charms that, in Fanny's eyes, gave him the virility, the resolve, and now that dazzled rush of sympathy sometimes wrought by love combined with pleasure, when the two happen to come together.

The situation was so fantastical for Fanny, her body responding so naturally, that she laughed even while trying to explain her laughter, and Ludovic, surprised, was then rapidly won over and conquered as he would have been by anything she could have said or done. Lying close to him, on her side, she made out the great height of this man, the dry sweetness of his skin, the breadth of his shoulders, his strength, in fact his self-possession too. And she gave not a thought to her age or his, in no way felt that an obstacle; it was just an unimportant fact like the difference in their hair color. He was wondering at each detail of her body, even her little flaws, as if each was a discovery and a gift. And this gaze resting on her so naturally, so indiscreetly, did not diminish her ease, any critical appraisal or shyness now no threat to her at all.

No more than the door which, five meters beyond them, opened onto the salons and a very likely scandal.

They got through the whole dinner with sweet and somewhat whitewashed faces and calm, lighthearted manners, which raised an alarm for Philippe. He could recognize the signs of pleasure, despite being so inexpert in those of love.

Henri was wearing a loose bandage on his right hand and kept knocking it on the peppermills, which meant swearing regularly under his breath, decorum forbidding his use of certain expressions in the presence of the three women: his guest, his daughter-in-law, and the ever-ceremonious Sandra.

"An accident at work thanks to that imbecile of a Tokyo importer who absolutely had to see our new pea-shelling machine, a marvel of technology, which cost us a mere two hundred thousand dollars!" he said, fearsomely brandishing his knife over Philippe and Ludovic, who gaped back at him. "While I was showing him that . . . bitch of a machine, I went a mite too close to the slicing blade . . . Hardly dinner conversation . . . Thing nicked my wrist."

And he thrust his bandage into the middle of the table.

"How dreadful!" Fanny exclaimed. "It could have been worse, I suppose?"

"Yes, indeed," Henri replied, somewhat mollified, and showed his teeth in a grimace of suffering.

"You ought to take better care, Father," Marie-Laure spoke up, though she was as indifferent to his distress as Sandra. "But what on earth was that Japanese man doing here in Touraine?"

"True," said Fanny, "so far from Tokyo. You ought to have invited him to dinner."

"There are seven delegates from the IAOPU—they're the biggest importers of grain in Japan and the whole of Asia."

"Seven!" said Ludovic, suddenly spurred into action. "What a bargain. Well, between them and this bothersome soirée that's coming up, we're quite the beating heart of commerce here!"

He let out a guffaw so relaxed that the rest of the table was stunned. Henri recovered his presence of mind and bad temper first, in part because Fanny was laughing too.

"Let me remind you, my boy, that we are holding this 'bothersome soirée' for you. To show our connections that you didn't come back from your hospitals quite as loony as we thought! Of which conclusion I'm not yet convinced, as it happens."

"It's certainly debatable," replied Ludovic, as buoyant as before.

"And I must add that, while you were playing the charming invalid with your nurses, I for one was working!"

This initiated a lengthy silence, and all eyes dropped to the tablecloth before the only mildly embarrassed Henri returned to his theme.

"Besides, I'm the only one around here who *does* any work. Apart from you, dear friend, of course," he said, seizing and heartily kissing Fanny's hand.

Ludovic's laughter rocketed out of control.

"But Papa, I had no luck with those nurses, you know. Such healthy, sturdy, energetic women they were," he added, turning to Fanny with a proper schoolboy laugh: insolent, imprudent, and with at least one eye on his audience.

"But you've made up for it now, haven't you?" Marie-Laure stepped in to ask. "With Madame Hamel's young employees? Or that's what I've heard."

*She actually hisses like a little viper*, thought Fanny, whose head was spinning. Furious, she got to her feet and snapped, "I find your conversation intolerable. I can't listen to any more, anyway. You'll have to excuse me."

And she walked out.

Philippe stood, politely, Ludovic stopped laughing, and Henri allowed a degree of confusion to register on his face. There had been moments of alignment, of complicity between Fanny and Ludovic, and then outrage from Fanny, all of which alarmed Philippe even more. And perhaps Marie-Laure too, for she now stood also and followed her mother—the first sign of family solidarity she had shown to date.

The three men remained. Henri muttered a few things, doubtless excuses but inaudible to the others. Then he stood up, rapped out a "Good night," which sounded like nothing so much as a "To bed!" and left the other two sitting face-to-face, Ludovic with his eyes fixed on the parquet and Philippe staring at Ludovic.

"Do you think it will be fine tomorrow?" Philippe asked. "And do you think the sun will shine for the soirée too?"

"I've no idea. No one has."

"Your lovely mother-in-law seems to be counting on its doing so. It must be said she's an optimistic lady. Sweetness incarnate, for her age."

"I have no notion of her age," Ludovic answered, smiling once more, as if in spite of himself, which rather ruffled his uncle's feathers.

Philippe had no personal feeling for Fanny, and despite her infinite politeness, he knew that she considered him like a photo, an immutable character, frozen in time; he sometimes felt the same himself.

# 8.

When Fanny saw Ludovic again, she no longer thought him a strange, ageless, characterless figure, much less a babe lost in the woods, but rather a man with whom she somehow, confusedly, belonged. The unsettling thing was his good humor, his lack of resentment and even of any riposte when people talked down to him with the implacable rancor of those who have subjected a person to a cruel humiliation and yet manage to blame him for it. His indulgence—or unawareness?—redoubled their mistrust. Fanny feared she would discover sordid reasons for this amnesia of his, material ones perhaps, and his fresh charm was rapidly fading in the face of this particular theory.

She had decided to think about it overnight, to pack and leave perhaps the next morning, and in any case to talk it through with Ludovic. But hardly had she lain down on her countrified bed—with her Evian water standing on her bedside table, looking on like a wise chaperone—before she was serenely asleep. And the only images to play behind her eyelids were of Ludovic's laughing face, his clear chestnut eyes alight with happiness. She couldn't understand herself. Back then, the moment she had set eyes on Quentin, with his English looks and his full mouth, she had loved and desired him. But Ludovic had prompted only a sense of compassion and curiosity at first. What had changed?

The fact remains that Fanny did not hear the pattering of small pebbles pitched against her shutters by her suitor. Doubtless it was better that way.

◆ ◆ ◆

When Fanny came into the dining room the following morning and saw Ludovic standing, looking toward the door, with the same eyes and smile of the evening before, she was surprised by his impatient, rapt expression. An unexpected surge of tenderness brought a lump to her throat; she stopped in the doorway, noting as she did so that Marie-Laure was facing away as she nibbled her melba toast so could not see Fanny's expression. Sitting down, Fanny felt guilty before her daughter for the first time ever, and she readied herself to create a scene about Ludovic as if he were an intruder or had raped her last night and made her pregnant. Why had she now complicated an already difficult situation, given the nature of the protagonists?

"Good morning!" Fanny said, smiling to the company with politeness born of unbreakable habit.

Various "good mornings" came in answer, including one from Philippe, whom she hadn't spotted, wrapped in his rather tired-looking dressing gown. Henri had already left for the factory, and Ludovic seemed waylaid by daydreams.

"Goodness, Mother, are you determined to submit to these hellish preparations?" Marie-Laure was looking approvingly at Fanny's velvet trousers and silk blouse.

"You ought to wear trousers more often," she added. "With your figure, they make you look even younger. Yes, they do!" she finished, as if someone were refuting her compliment.

Fanny smiled genuinely. "You think so?"

Adopting a concerned expression, she gave her daughter an affectionate appraisal and declared, "As for you, my darling, keep away from trousers. You have always been charming with your slim waist, those little pleated skirts, and your pointy shoes."

"Well, I shall go and change in any case," said Marie-Laure, furiously, gesturing to her Chanel skirt suit. "I'm about to go for a round of golf."

It was rather hard for her to have Fanny snub her outfit while Ludovic, who admired her style despite his egregious infidelities, had eyes only for her mother. Fanny was indeed looking very young that day, and hinting at an imperceptible age did not necessarily play as she would have liked. She rose.

Since her husband's return, Marie-Laure had been spending many afternoons playing golf and thereby catching up with some old friends from abroad, "miraculously escaped from the Ritz," as she put it, to whom she explained Ludovic's whereabouts as "rehab," a vague but unsettling term that best legitimized his absence, which in truth was exactly as she liked it. She was enjoying sighing over her admirer, an American with a substantial although unprestigious fortune. After three years of virtual widowhood, she was not going to settle for a manufacturer from Minnesota. After golf, Marie-Laure would return to La Cressonnade to call her friends, as she did every day, but also, as every day, to call Messrs. Perez and Seiné, the defenders present and future of her inheritance, that is, of her portion of the Cresson fortune. She also liked to spend an hour chatting to Philippe, with whom she'd had several discussions since the escapades of Cressons junior and senior had come to light.

◆  ◆  ◆

That day, Ludovic's convertible, the one given him by his father upon his return from convalescence, awaited him and Fanny below the terrace. Ludovic took the steps in a single leap.

"We mustn't forget the flowers for Marie-Laure!" he called out. "I told everyone we're off to do some shopping."

He seemed delighted with his duplicity. What was Fanny doing with this backward boy? He had told her that he loved her madly, had made love to her the way she liked it, and had been a renowned rake for years. What did she want of him? Not to lose respect for him. But anyway, what right had she to that?

The station was no distance away. She had only to catch a train to avoid some conduct or reaction that risked making her ridiculous.

"Do you have the keys?" he asked.

"Yes," she replied briefly, then fumbled in her handbag and located them.

She tossed them over to him with the passenger door already open and sat down inside. He had already asked to drive if . . . and she had accepted the idea; now he peered into the windshield, face already a mask of anxiety. But she did not demur. The last fortnight had created a kind of rule, yet the hints of a man who had possessed her and said he loved her could not be interpreted any other way. Nor, especially, should he let his own wife treat him like a buffoon in front of her and let her commandeer the wheel from dawn to dusk. At first Fanny had pitied him, but now, sitting beside this young man ultimately without any responsibilities, she felt sorry for herself, she who worked for her living, who lived without her husband and had devoted her holiday to this family of cold-blooded bourgeoisie.

"What's wrong?"

"Let's go, and take it easy, Ludovic, I'm tired. You have the wheel."

She let her head drop back and closed her eyes.

After a moment's silence, Fanny heard Ludovic sit down beside her, put the car in gear, start the engine, and set off smoothly, without a jolt. She kept her eyes closed as an indication of her confidence but also, mainly, her weariness.

"I've no idea where the windshield wipers are," said a cheery, almost triumphant voice. "I just can't remember."

She opened her eyes, for a moment gazed on her manservant with his worried yet innocent eyes on hers, and with her left hand set the wipers going.

"You're not afraid to go with me? I didn't dare ask, but I've been practicing in secret ever since you arrived."

"Not at all," she said. "Why should I be?"

And she closed her eyes again.

Ludovic drove in silence as far as Tours, the city of temptations, where he did his manservant turn in each of the shops, pushing shopping carts and looking upon each transaction with an approving eye. He was surrounded by a crowd of salesladies who'd gotten overexcited by Madame Hamel's elliptical accounts of her meeting with the young Monsieur Cresson. The possibly insane gentleman seemed to be waiting hand and foot upon his mother-in-law, who appeared as pleasant as his own wife was unbearable.

They found themselves in the middle of a large department store, and Fanny was hesitating over the porcelain tureen she would set on each table when she showed him the total bill.

"What do you think?"

"Oh," he said without even looking, "free rein is free rein. And does it matter so much?" he added, tugging her by the sleeve toward an exit. "It's just to impress the local people who'll choose the same thing for their own parties, you'll see."

"But I shan't be at their parties," Fanny replied, laughing, as he sat her back in the car and busied himself following her orders, packing everything into the trunk and revealing the opposite of that young man obscured by medication and apathy or trampled on by his nearest and dearest.

As Fanny was being re-imprisoned in their uncomfortable machine, in the middle of the street, he leaned over and pressed his lips to her hair, very rapidly and openly. She sat up straight in her seat.

"Now, Ludovic Cresson, you really are mad! What will they say in Tours?"

"Whatever they like. In any case, we will go traveling, won't we? I've hardly seen the world. Assuming you like to travel, of course."

She sank back in her seat. At that moment, she would have given anything for access to a hotel bedroom with door and key—even in Tours, which she disliked—where she might lock herself in, reclaim a normal life, and find her way back to Paris and her very own Cressonnade, all one hundred square meters of it. *Well*, she thought. *What is wrong with me? What a scene! Like an idiot I show up for three weeks in the country to help out my exasperating daughter, and I'm stupid enough to yield to this boy who's victimized by his family, and now we're having a love affair that's doomed from the start?*

Once, after Quentin's death, Fanny had spent a night with someone who had humiliated her the next day with his air of conquest and his preening. Who had, more precisely, dishonored her sense of love, forever inspired by Quentin's example, which depended on respect for the other person. Around her she had seen distinguished wits behave like boors with their wives or mistresses and charming women wax lyrical about their lovers' prowess for the benefit of their hairdressers. In those days a kind of inverted puritanism masquerading as liberty had been the rule, which astonished her when she discovered it, for Quentin and his sensibility had so far shielded her from it. Now a vision was panicking her like some fundamental fault line: a general incapacity for love overlaid by a frenzied urge to advertise one's affairs.

◆ ◆ ◆

Fanny and Ludovic spent the afternoon weaving through the streets of Tours, buying essential items in accordance with a list compiled three days earlier and in a serious hand by Fanny, which now seemed to her as incoherent as it was unrealistic. She chatted about the weather, plans for the party, the prevailing fashion in Tours, and Ludovic answered her with equal levity, no pressure. When she looked at him, she discovered his haggard face, filled with questions and convinced of his own guilt. His bewilderment over the crime committed kept him silent; his incomprehension and anguish aged and even slightly disfigured him. There was nothing left of the happy, innocent young lover of the day before. Once more he was alone, desperate and suddenly adult—but adult in the way that pain matures you; as if locked in the corner of a room, of a life, your back to all hopes of a future; alone—still alone, just alone. Yesterday Ludovic had thought he was breaking out of the loneliness but now, already bound to Fanny, he had no resources left.

He attracted her and she trembled. The beauty of his skin, his long, lowered eyelashes, his restless eyes, the shapes of his big hands on the wheel—such oddly solid hands, which she now knew to be skilled and thoughtful too. All that she had discovered the day before now made her look away, as she had in the most ardent moments of her love for Quentin.

The more she thought about it, the more shocked and worried she felt. It wasn't possible to become so intimate, so naturally close to someone, from the very first embrace. They had come together in some parallel space, fearlessly, without curiosity or reticence. She could not help but credit destiny, even though she was ten years older, give or take, even if it was a scandal, even if he was unstable, even if all her habits and the life she had built repudiated this bond, those two hours at the piano.

# 9.

At the table that evening, the conversation limped. Henri wondered why tourists were so determined to visit the same places, and he seemed particularly exercised by Notre-Dame Cathedral, which he found lumpen, boring, and overelaborate.

"Besides," he added, "those god-awful head things sticking out everywhere . . . What do they call them again, those horrors stuck onto the outside? So appalling. What do you call them?"

"Gargoyles," said Ludovic.

"How do *you* know that?" asked Henri, astonished, as if his son had revealed some terrifying atomic secret.

"Yes, indeed," Marie-Laure said. "Where did you come across this knowledge? The gargoyles we used to see were never made of stone, as far as I thought."

"Oh, there was one—I married her."

Ludovic's supremely calm words were followed by an interminable silence. Henri flushed with satisfaction and was opening his mouth to give his opinion, doubtless misplaced yet conclusive, when they heard a slow and heavy tread make its way over their heads. They sat motionless, forks lifted, eyes wide. The room above belonged to Sandra, who'd been barred from verticality for some time and was confined to bed with a night nurse at her side as skinny as her diurnal counterpart was vast.

"So we have Hamlet, hearing his father's footsteps in act 1," Ludovic said, on something of a roll.

"I ask you!" shouted Henri, on his feet in a shot. "She must lie down this minute. Dr. Murat . . . Marat . . . I don't recall—he was categorical about this yesterday. Philippe, go up and get her back in bed. I'm right behind you. Off you go, old man, on the double!"

Philippe leapt toward the staircase, looking more zealous than anxious.

Marie-Laure was slowly recovering from Ludovic's pronouncement.

"What can be up with her?" Henri wondered aloud, referring to his wife.

Marie-Laure broke in. "Look, Father, your wife has been trotting about her bedroom all this last week. She wants to surprise you at the party."

"Surely not!" Henri's consternation was unmistakable. "She can't do that . . . She has no right! Even Doctor Whatsisname, there, at the Hôtel-Dieu hospital, he told me—"

"She doesn't care, Father."

"But she looks . . . She's the color of an overripe tomato," Henri thundered, "a raw leg of lamb . . . She'll faint over the dessert or Lord knows what else! Ah no, no, no, no! And what about Fanny? Fanny will be receiving the guests, won't she? I've told all my friends that, for once, a pretty woman will be hostess at La Cressonnade!" And he muttered rapidly, "Sandra has other qualities, of course."

"You can't speak of your wife like that," Fanny said, shocked. "First of all, I am handing the crown back to its rightful owner, with pleasure . . . Then, the terms by which you express yourself."

"But there was no ill will meant," Henri attempted to excuse himself. "And besides, it's true . . . well, you know how men are." He gave a small sharkish smirk, which really did not suit him. "Mere words, that's all," he insisted, with his usual insincerity. "Don't tell me you've never heard a man talk of lamb both raw and cooked in reference to his wife! Perhaps inaccurately, now and then, but without vulgarity."

"I have not," Fanny replied firmly. "Cooked or uncooked, I have never heard a husband compare his wife to a leg of lamb."

At this she giggled nervously and was obliged to leave the table at top speed, maintaining a lofty expression.

"Never," she shouted, already on the stairs. "Never!"

On the landing she actually broke into a slow trot all the way to her room.

The remaining three, Marie-Laure, Ludovic, and Henri, found themselves sitting together, ears strained ceilingward, looking rather ridiculous. The overhead pacing had stopped.

"Martin," Henri asked, as if the other two at the table were quite deaf, "you can't hear it anymore, now, can you?"

"No, monsieur," the butler replied, and presented the cheese board, which Henri pushed away in exasperation.

"But you did hear them, the footsteps, a moment ago?"

"No, monsieur," Martin said, in the same neutral tone.

The two men stared at each other in fierce antipathy.

"Take this cheese out of my sight! Nobody wants any!"

Marie-Laure, even though she detested cheese, waved a dissenting hand at the butler, but a glance at her father-in-law changed her mind and she set her hand back on the table.

"Anyway," Henri said, "Philippe is a good influence on his sister: she's gone back to bed!"

"Unless he knocked her out with a wrench?" Ludovic suggested.

Marie-Laure looked at him with an amused smile for the first time since his homecoming—though Ludovic did not return it. He was watching his father keenly: Henri was visibly hesitating between his duty to Sandra and the mad desire to get away from her. Suddenly decisive, he strode away to the cloakroom. Ludovic and his wife sat for a moment looking at each other, then both rose and left. As for Philippe, he did not reappear—and was therefore unable to enjoy the family's compliments on his diplomacy.

◆ ◆ ◆

At eleven that evening, Sylvia Hamel was ensconced in her little doily-lined drawing room where two of her protégées, one on a divan, the other an armchair, were pouring out their woes. One had just seen a new and sexually wayward client, from whom she had simply had to run away. "Tourists and strangers: never!" Madame Hamel nonetheless continued to caution her, while proffering a bandage for her twisted ankle. Equally upset by her fright, the other girl was watching trustingly as, enthroned at her little desk, Madame Hamel replied decisively to a letter received that very morning by her tenant, which letter, sent by a former friend, had the nerve to claim two months' worth of the girl's earnings. Madame Hamel's face, as she recited the impressive list of her official guardians and protectors, could have put off any number of upstart would-be pimps.

It was into this tense scene that Henri Cresson made his entrance—but that suited him perfectly. Bared limbs, champagne, and knowing winks would have exasperated him. He asked Madame Hamel to accord him a little of her time and advice right away, for he had again appreciated her recent discretion and good sense. Besides, for some time now, he added, he'd been wanting to upgrade the harmonium organ at Saint-Eustache church (the centerpiece of Madame Hamel's realm), an improvement stingy contributions had so far not enabled. Madame Hamel put a stop to his protracted digressions, folded the letter, and sent both unhappy young women away before carefully closing the door to the hall.

Surrounded by doilies, Henri looked like a bull who'd been heroically but imprudently decorated and freed before ever having set foot in the ring. He downed two brandies in a row, then asked his valued old friend, "Here's the thing. You are aware that, having been laid low recently by one of her fainting fits, Sandra is bedbound on doctor's orders. So it is that my sister-in-law . . . I mean, a relative . . . well, my daughter-in-law's mother has very kindly agreed to host our party alongside my son and me. And Madame Fanny Crawley is a delightful lady."

"Indeed," said Madame Hamel. "I happened to meet her at the Trois Dauphins. She was buying wicker chairs for your party and she seemed very pleasant, elegant and Parisian. And she looks so young . . . How old is she?"

"Why, I haven't the foggiest," Henri realized. "No matter: in my view, she's a handsome young lady, charming, lively, and attractive. Very, very attractive."

"Unquestionably," Madame Hamel agreed, beginning to be rather surprised.

"She works in Paris for a very well-known designer whose name I don't recall. An admirable position, of course, but it doesn't provide well for her."

He paused, then added, "In fact, I mean to marry her."

Sylvia Hamel, who in one evening had offered refuge to two petrified girls, now saw the region's principal manufacturer—provider of employment for hundreds of local people and thereby, from her point of view, furnisher of hundreds of clients—apparently losing his mind. Was he drunk? She rose from her armchair.

"Monsieur Cresson," she said in her deepest register, "are you not married?"

"For far too long!" exclaimed Henri in turn, likewise leaping to his feet. "My wife is a virago; you know that. The whole town knows it. There is such a thing as divorce, for God's sake!"

He sat down again.

Madame Hamel poured herself a brandy. "Does she know it?"

She was thinking of Sandra, but Henri did not share her priorities.

"No . . . Fanny doesn't know, nor does Sandra, or anyone else. I wanted your advice."

The initial shock behind her, Madame Hamel was recovering her composure.

"Believe me when I say I'm deeply flattered . . . The first to know: truly, such an honor. Well, if I understand correctly, no action has yet been taken?"

"It will be, in the next few days," Henri replied.

"But has Madame . . . I mean, has your daughter-in-law's mother said yes?"

"Not yet. I've not mentioned it to her as such, but these things, you know, one tends to sense . . ."

And he assumed an expression of long psychological experience, which did not go far in convincing Madame Hamel.

"I had thought of making the announcement at our party, with all the guests, except for Sandra, of course—she'll be in her room . . . Two pieces of good news alongside dessert: my son is not mad, and I'm marrying a superb woman."

He seemed genuinely enchanted.

"My God," Madame Hamel said.

And she thought, *He's the crazy one!*

"As for Ludovic, the poor kid has been deprived of a mother, and he has great affection for Fanny."

Recalling her girls' unanimous and comprehensive approval of Ludovic's amorous approaches, then remembering too the latter's personal charm, Madame Hamel let herself sink deeper into her armchair, eyes half closed, feigning sage rumination of the situation while, in her mind's eye—which was little used to such extravagance—she pictured a succession of incestuous duels, bloodthirsty murders, and more.

"Even so, if I were you, Monsieur Cresson, I would wait until a few days after the party before deciding all of this. Madame Cresson—Sandra—must not be the last to hear of it."

"They do say the penny drops last for the dupe . . . Oh, do forgive me . . . This is the one little flaw Fanny complains of in me: my colorful expressions."

And he had such a self-satisfied expression that she couldn't help adding, "It's a small thing, that's true. But has she not, herself, other connections in Paris?"

"I'll take care of it," Henri replied, drawing himself to his full, hawkish height.

The cognac bottle now practically empty, Madame Hamel and Henri exchanged toasts and best wishes, and she took her chance to add, "Don't you think that, instead of marrying your delightful Fanny, you might guarantee her a glorious and care-free life in Paris without causing dramas, provoking your wife's ire, and setting all and sundry talking about you?"

"Fanny is not mistress material, Madame Hamel! She is the kind of woman one marries first."

"Perhaps if you were to spend six months with her before-hand, to consolidate your understanding . . . And you know, between a divorce and a remarriage there must be a gap of three hundred days."

"We shall be married in Tahiti or Andorra, or in Luxembourg—the mayor is a friend."

"Does she like the countryside?" asked Madame Hamel, wobbling slightly (from the brandy or the psychological impact).

Henri hesitated. "She confessed to me that she would find it prettier if the exterior and interior of the house were in harmony."

He stood once more, detached a loose doily suspended from his trousers, and took Madame Hamel's hand and kissed it.

"Heavens, it is two in the morning . . . My sincerest apologies . . . Thank you once more for your good advice."

But which advice was that, out of the long evening's worth Madame Hamel had offered? She was so tired and discombobulated that she forgot to remind him about the harmonium at Saint-Eustache.

# 10.

Deeply unsettled, Fanny had slid into bed in all her clothes. It had rained during dinner but the blue-black sky, overrun by a thousand tiny drenched and huddled stars, stretched out beyond her window. She stood there a couple of minutes, hearing nothing but the peaceable wind slowing, rocking the plane leaves, sometimes laying them against each other like prayer-book pages turned by a diligent pastor. Then she undressed and took a bath, repeating aloud several times: "Raw leg of lamb—no, absolutely never!" And she saw herself standing there, again, unbending before poor Henri trying to reframe his words as comical, although the expression really was more incongruous than it was mean. And she dissolved into giggles once more.

At four in the morning, the hall door creaked and Ludovic slipped into Fanny's bedroom. He was still wearing his clothes from that day—a smart decision. For had he arrived ready to go, shaved and aftershaved, in a fine dressing gown, primped and primed in his lover's role, Fanny would have shown him the door instantly. Instead, when she turned her bedside lamp on, she saw him standing haggard and lost on the far side of her room, by the window, and apparently readier to jump out of that than into her bed.

"Ludovic." She whispered instinctively, although the next nearest bedroom was Philippe's, two rooms along, and, despite his adventurous past, even if his door were left open, Philippe had a snore like a combine harvester.

Ludovic was unkempt, with the same brown mohair sweater pulled over his crumpled shirt. His favorite sweater, Fanny thought, surprised at her knowledge of the young man's wardrobe. Indeed, this brown sweater, his soft red shirt, his corduroy trousers, and almost-new slippers were all precisely as she recalled them. She motioned for him to sit.

"It is four in the morning, Ludovic. You've not undressed or changed . . . or been to bed?"

At first lighthearted, her voice slowed despite her efforts as she lost interest in what she was saying. He waved a hand to stop her, almost rudely, or it would have been rude from Henri.

"I have come to say that if I upset or shocked you, it was a mistake. Since this morning, I have been trying . . . all I find is your eyes and the freshness of your voice. I am terribly unhappy—that's all."

With those last few words, he looked up directly at her.

"Listen," he added. "I wasn't thinking that you loved me too, not yet, but that you liked me a good deal and that we were getting on."

"And that's true," she said.

For it *was* true that she liked him, almost lying there at her feet.

Fanny spoke again. "I have never loved anyone but Quentin, my husband. Apart from everything else, he protected me; I was safe from the world, from other people . . . Now I live alone. I don't earn very much, and I still need protecting; do you see?"

He nodded. His eyes were fixed on her, but in no way awkwardly.

"Now here, the one who needs protecting is you, from all these people," she said, making an encompassing gesture, "who did everything to you, who make fun of you, don't trust you, and denigrate you when they should be asking your forgiveness every day . . . my daughter first of all . . . You see, I've no wish for a son or a lover kneeling here."

He stood up to go back out by the window.

"You're right," he said in a strangled voice. "But they frightened me . . . They still frighten me. What if they send

116

me back there? Marie-Laure said just one phone call . . . And when I was in there, they were the only people I knew on the outside, the only ones I thought were trying to get me out, the only ones who came to see me, do you understand? My father, my wife, and my mother-in-law . . . Without them, I would probably still be there."

There was a silence. Fanny got up. "But it was the doctors who discharged you."

Then something snapped inside her. She enunciated "Ludovic," probably with some kind of summoning gesture for, the next moment, he was in her arms, kissing her tears though she hardly felt their flow, consoling her for all that had been done to *him* and that she found unbearable.

"Oh my dear," she said, presently, with a gentleness that Ludovic's kisses and his hands turned, at first little by little and then hastily, into urgent embraces.

A lamp turned out, the sweater a woman tears over a man's burning head, the shirt he rips off himself; trousers, shoes tossed one after the other; words of love, tears shared, a mouth held to another mouth. Then the sound of two bodies falling one upon the other, of two leaves, two pages . . . and the wind, the wind rising with the day.

# 11.

Henri Cresson had returned to the sanctuary of his house and even that of his wife, slinking in by a small hallway door that led straight into his own bathroom. He reached his bedroom on tiptoe, as well as one can tiptoe after a certain number of cognacs and some great excitement. The breathing of his wife, who had lovingly or reprovingly left their communicating doors half open, reached him in a rhythm of alternating snores and whistles. And this exemplary confidence and well-being inspired in Henri a kind of good-natured, preemptive regret, something like shame.

He went over to his desk, which was modern in outward style but had been built by his grandfather Antoine Cresson, a keen cabinetmaker and secret keeper. If you pressed the top edge of a drawer while pushing it in, and at the same time gave a robust kick to one of the desk legs, you triggered the release of a third drawer, where lay a testament in repose all the more peaceful for a copy of the same document's also lying comfortably in the safes of Messrs. Locone & Locone Fils, notaries in Paris. Henri laid the pages on his bed, undressed, and set about rewriting them.

◆ ◆ ◆

The next day, Fanny went out to buy a few things, not in Tours but all the way to Orléans, where her anonymity was assured. There she picked up a copy of *Alienation from Society: Mental Health and the Law*, among other books, which she leafed through in a café before setting off back to La Cressonnade. She underlined sections on several pages and upon her return left them on Ludovic's bed. She shivered for a moment crossing her daughter's bedroom and seeing her comfort, her luxury, the various accoutrements she had brought back from Paris. A floor down, Ludovic's room looked like a soldier's cell—almost uninhabited in comparison, even though he'd lived in it and still did. Then she recalled the tone her daughter used to speak of Ludovic, still her husband, after all, with whom she had shared a bed and some years, and whom she now treated like an object of no value, while Fanny herself had firsthand experience of his charms as a lover.

Citing lunch with an old friend in Orléans, Fanny had left amid general concern: Philippe suspicious because he looked for lies everywhere, Ludovic sorry because he would miss her and because a lie from Fanny would have been a deadly cruelty to him, and Henri unnerved, for he couldn't imagine what she might find to do anywhere farther away than Tours.

With Fanny away, at two o'clock that afternoon Ludovic went into her bedroom and straight to her bed. She had made it, drawing the sheets high, and it was only on pulling them back that he could see the rumpling and creases of their long night. The shutters stood open, and a few of Fanny's clothes remained scattered about, among them her nightgown in the bathroom. It seemed to Ludovic to be waiting for her: pale pink, long, and crushed over the back of a chair in such a way as no nightgown had ever or would again await her. He laid his cheek on it, lifted it up to his hair, and pressed his face into it.

He physically jumped when someone coughed behind him. He turned to find Martin there, Martin with his expression impassive as ever—or imbecilic, depending on your view. Oddly, with many years and many silences behind them, Ludovic had a soft spot for the butler, seeing him as an inoffensive creature, unlike the other members of his family. They exchanged a long look, and Ludovic was sorry he'd made such a point of this now, flagged his "guilt" so clearly, but it was too late and he slowly laid the nightdress back on the chair.

"It's a lovely fabric," he said, regretfully, as if he would really have liked the same for himself.

A reflection of his regret passing over the bemused Martin's face made Ludovic give a sudden giggle. He picked up the nightdress and held it in front of Martin's torso, which, with his bald head and immovable solemnity, did not make him look any better in the mirror. After a moment's contemplation, without a flicker of movement in his face, Martin gave the object of Ludovic's dreams back to him.

"It will look very fine," he said to Ludovic, somewhat stunned.

Ludovic had not noticed the striking, if sophisticated, odor that betrayed the presence of his stepmother wherever she appeared, like *Aïda*'s trumpets. Decked out in a leaf-pattern dressing gown, this lady stood framed in the doorway, followed closely by her enormous daytime nurse with visible disapproval.

"Which of you two intends to sport this pastel shade?" Sandra said, without a smile. "Is it for the party?"

Ludovic and Martin spoke over each other in their rush to reassure her.

"Look here, no one . . . It's just a little joke! I was saying to Martin he must have looked adorable in this color at his baptism. He is still rather adorable, in fact, with his cherubic looks . . ."

Ludovic was digging himself into a hole, and Sandra gave the butler a quick once-over to check whether any childishness had affected the appearance of the mulish steward she knew so well.

"Be that as it may, he'd have worn blue, I imagine. He has always been a boy, childish or not. Right . . ." she went on, sighing, then turned back to Ludovic to ask, "Has your mother gone out?"

"My mother?" he repeated, in surprise, seeing one already standing before him.

"Yes! Not me, of course. I mean Fanny, your mother-in-law, your wife's, Marie-Laure's, mother."

"Ah, of course . . ." Ludovic smiled. "Of course."

He was trying, prompted by Martin, to extract himself from the bathroom, but his stepmother was blocking the door. Although somewhat attenuated over the last three days, her high pink color nonetheless evoked fauvist art more than impressionist paintings.

"Fanny, of course . . . Fanny. It's strange; I wasn't thinking of her as a relative," Ludovic said.

"Excuse me, madame," the butler intervened, having reached the door and sensing indefinable dangers hovering all around.

"Are you in a hurry, Martin? Does neither of you wish to explain what you intend to do with all this pink? To hell with it! This bedroom looks very empty indeed," Sandra concluded with a censorious headshake. "I know poor Fanny hasn't a hundred square meters to herself in Paris, but to give her this room, and after all the furniture I offered her! I ask you . . ."

# 12.

The sky had shifted to a pale blue, but the next day it was azure. And the palette of Sandra's face had shifted to a stormy blue more reminiscent of repeated batterings than of raw meat. Encouraged by her fine profile's resumption of less bloody hues, she had decreed a game of bridge for the afternoon, inviting Fanny and Marie-Laure to her room (the men of the house being dyed-in-the-wool anti-bridgers), even though her two guests were rather poor players of a game they had not practiced for years. The Queen—whom they called by the name she used: Madame de Boyau, "the name passed down from her great-uncle Louis the Sixteenth," Sandra said, adding, "thus keeping her safe from the guillotines"—would stand in as the fourth player.

Despite ideas involving walks and countryside, Ludovic discovered himself deprived of Fanny.

The three bridge players sat on the bed around Sandra, herself well propped among her pillows and comfortably facing her somewhat higgledy-piggledy fellow players. Naturally, while knocking a tennis ball against the next wall in an effort to calm down, Ludovic sent a ball right through Sandra's window, smashing that along with her charming Huguenot statuettes. He was roundly rebuked by Sandra and the poor, now disheveled Queen, and was scolded by his wife, all under the amused gaze of Fanny, which helped make up for the rest of the punishment. He headed out into the woods while Henri went on with his siesta.

The bridge party went off without further incident. The Queen could be found at bridge at all hours and was in the habit of returning bent double with the weight of her winnings to the fine villa of her husband, Villabois, which she viewed as her final stop before acceding to the throne. She was, then, under the illusion that these two Parisian newbies would be guaranteeing the pay of her Swiss guards. Marie-Laure and Fanny were partners, and Sandra and the Queen made up the other pair. However, for this royal game, Fanny played two hours of flamboyantly excellent bridge, decisive play after decisive play, from which her infuriated highness could not recover despite repeated attempts to regain the upper hand, all in vain.

At about eight in the evening, while Sandra muttered crossly, an amused and delighted Marie-Laure openly counted her and her mother's winnings.

"My goodness," Fanny said, "what a fabulous game! That makes three months' rent paid in Paris, thanks to a queen of clubs alone," referring to her final spectacular hand.

Exiled, ruined, disillusioned, and tight-lipped, the Queen paid up, said good evening, and departed in short order.

"We shan't be her ladies of honor at the coronation, shall we," Fanny said, chuckling.

"I wasn't the one leading that unholy game," Sandra snapped.

"No, but it comes to ten thousand francs all the same," Marie-Laure added, determined to overcome her mother-in-law's reluctance to honor her debt.

The latter was obliged to comply.

Marie-Laure added, "And I must thank you, Mother; you were the best partner one could wish for."

"Happy at play, unhappy in love," Sandra growled.

Which triggered a fit of giggles from Ludovic's mother-in-law, for reasons unknown to her fellow players. She even had to excuse herself abruptly and run all the way back to the refuge of her room.

Ludovic knocked at Fanny's door before the bell sounded. She realized that her gift of law books had sent him to sleep more than anything else. He seemed to feel that the harm he'd been done now fell to her to rectify, and for a moment she was deeply discouraged. Sheltered all her life, only taking charge following Quentin's death and then not without difficulty, Fanny had not imagined that she would also be obliged to defend the rights of this full-grown boy who would surely, one day, be engaged in such defenses himself. This family's mindset entailed a danger worse than any other: Ludovic might be sent back, on some pretext or other, to one of those hells of peace and quiet from which he had emerged. This was why he looked away and avoided all conversations that might lead to the famous and imminent soirée, which already seemed terrifying due to the number of guests—or strangers, actually—the number of people there to judge him, ready to support any move Sandra might make against him. His father's lack of interest was hardly reassuring.

Fanny realized sadly that even with Sandra back on her feet, even a healthy, rosy-pink Sandra would not relieve her of her duty to protect this odd, reckless, and disarming young lover. The only drive that motivated Ludovic was his passion for her, and yet, aged thirty-odd, he was still obliged to hide it as if he were a boy. Fanny, exquisite, irreproachable Fanny, found herself suddenly responsible for and guilty of the most unlikely middle-class comedy.

Nonetheless, she had time to describe the royal bridge game to Ludovic with much hilarity and, having made him laugh, herself ended up weeping with laughter. She rebuked herself as soon as she was calm; she never had been able to count on the duration or the thoughtfulness of her own feelings. She had always tripped from one mood to the next, and her only lasting sentiments had been happy ones. "Therein lies her charm," Quentin used to say.

And she still had no idea that she had ignited the passion of the Hawk on High—the master of the house and her lover's father—and that these few weeks dedicated to duty had turned her into a femme fatale. That all this was happening in Tours instead of Paris lent an unreal aspect to the world beyond and all its flaws. But this sense of inconsequentiality was, as she knew, quite mistaken.

They were the last to arrive for dinner. Fanny and Ludovic laughed together as they came down the steps, Ludovic's hand on his mother-in-law's elbow, so responsible and protective was he with her. The other diners, disapproving of this late and laid-back entrance, gave them suspicious looks that might have suggested or indeed stirred some culpability. Fanny had the giggles for a moment, behavior that was poorly viewed in this dining room where, besides, the dog Ganache had surreptitiously chosen to lie under Ludovic's chair.

"You're last!" called Henri, nonetheless standing gallantly for Fanny. "Philippe, do you know whether your sister—my wife—lost a little color today?"

"Sandra is no longer at all flushed," Fanny said, reassuringly. "She has turned rather pale, in fact, even somewhat blueish, and tomorrow . . ."

She listened to her pleasant voice and was shocked at her words.

"Tomorrow," Henri stepped in, "if you have genuinely managed to address my wife's and our poor Queen's shameless cheating, Sandra will have turned yellow."

"The house rules here seem very untrustworthy to me," Philippe remarked. "I know what I'm talking about, thank God. In my youth, I played poker for an entire night with Jack Warner, the king of Hollywood cinema and poker. Did I ever tell you about it?"

Without waiting for a reply—which would, of course, be negative, for he was making this tale up there and then—he went on.

"There were three sharks in on the game, the three kings of Hollywood, in fact, who only accepted my joining their table after they'd laid bets on which of them would crush me, would squeeze me hardest. I got on a lot of nerves in Hollywood!" He chuckled. "I wasn't looking for parts; I was in love with a fabulously pretty but stone-broke lady; I had my own money. To cut a long story short—"

That word "short" retained no meaning for him, but Philippe was nonetheless cut short midstory by Ganache, to whom Ludovic, bored and recrossing his legs for the tenth time, had just delivered a gentle kick. The creature yapped, to general consternation, and the anecdote was interrupted. Hence, doubtless, Henri Cresson's unexpected reaction.

"Oh, you lovely doggy. Where have you popped up from? Have you adopted us on the sly? You're right: this is a fine house to live in. Isn't it, Fanny?" he inquired, and his smile of seduction chilled her to the bone.

"It's the best house you could choose," Fanny corroborated, stroking Ganache, who wagged his tail in delight; he was doing a round of the table and introducing himself to each diner in turn.

He carefully skirted Philippe and Marie-Laure, as if their disdain was sniffable, but lingered sensibly at Henri's feet— sensibly for, following his initial relief and gratification, Henri was already imagining Sandra's squawks and recriminations as she panicked over all her *objets*.

*I am getting a divorce, though*, he thought, *and Fanny seems to like dogs. What a woman! Ah, what a woman!*

He looked down at Ganache, and the joy and affection that he read in the dog's eyes made an agreeable change from the never-ending calculations in Sandra's. Ah, how alone he had been in this house, he thought. Tears rose unexpectedly to his eyes—tears for himself.

"Good little dog," he said, crouching over the animal to hide his emotion. "What's your name? What is this dog's name, Martin?" he suddenly yelled, to cover his weakness, though with the same disingenuousness. "His name, someone? Don't tell me you would allow an unknown animal to share my roof!"

"Ganache, monsieur," Martin replied coolly.

This poker-faced introduction was tailed by a sudden sparkling giggle from Fanny. Her laughter had been suppressed, she realized, ever since her arrival here, this genuine laughter in the grand and extravagant salons of La Cressonnade, which, in medieval times, would have crumbled at the sound of such a blasphemy.

Martin stalked back to his kitchen, scandalized by the sight of his master's emotion over a dirty, thieving dog. For the first time since beginning his service at the house, he thought gratefully of Sandra, who would put Ganache outside.

He had no time to ruminate any further on Sandra's merits before Henri's imperious voice was already calling him back to the dining room like one of those cartoon characters, bearing the desserts aloft. The diners seemed tired, even Henri, although Fanny's irresistible and contagious mirth had put everyone more at ease. Henri, the "Hawk suitor," felt neither sufficient energy nor of a mood to tell Fanny that evening the news of his own divorce and of their remarriage—to each other.

Henri's emotion over Ganache had disconcerted him. Fatigue had played its part too; also the wine, nerves, the royal bridge game, the dog's appearance, and enforced listening to tales of poker nights with Warner Bros. to cap it all. They had forgotten to applaud Philippe's Hollywood triumph due to the lack of a conclusion; even so, everyone suddenly felt wiped out.

So Henri lit a cigar, which he guessed would be his last of the day. Philippe didn't smoke, but Ludovic had brought some very odd cigarettes back from his last psychiatric residency; they must have been kept for the patients and stank alternately of eucalyptus and marmalade. The privileged few to have tried them smoked them down to the butt but never took a second.

No, Henri would wait another day to inform Fanny about her future. Despite all this, he kissed her hand ardently and whispered "Trust me" into her ear, which, as a true woman of the world, she found quite astonishing.

"Good night," he said. And then, to Ludovic: "Ah, I was forgetting. It seems you have demolished your stepmother's window."

"He just missed cutting the Queen's head off," said Fanny, laughing again. "We had lain her down by Sandra, the red queen and the white—"

"So who's telling tales on me?" Ludovic asked suddenly, frowning.

Assuming a pious expression, Martin directed his stare at Philippe.

"I was asleep," Philippe said, haughtily.

"So who was it?" Ludovic said again.

Marie-Laure blushed in anger and shame. Already a noted tattler at secondary school, in the last years of high school she had been iced out by her classmates over some tale-telling affair.

"You know," said Fanny, stepping in quickly, "the Tours chamber orchestra would be delighted to come and play at our soirée."

Henri shrugged. "Did they seem adequate to you? I could have some fashionable musicians brought over from Hollywood or Las Vegas, you know. And there's always Philippe's pipes."

"The Tours ensemble seemed very good to me," Ludovic said. "I dropped in on them yesterday."

"And I," Henri barked back, "I had them come to the factory; they played in the meeting room, very nicely and in time, and with some gusto too."

"If they overdo the gusto, the Venus de Milo will go to pieces," Fanny said with a smile. "Already she trembles in the slightest breeze. She's a danger to our guests. In fact, it may be her arm that is unbalancing her."

*She's thinking of everything*, Henri realized, with a wave of tenderness.

"I don't understand you," said Marie-Laure, furiously.

"The poor woman has only half an arm—you didn't know?" said Philippe, gleefully.

She stood up. "Yes, I did know. Stop trying to teach me everything, Philippe."

And despite smiles from Fanny and the rest of the diners, being highly sensitive over her own education—especially as it had in fact been somewhat superficial—Marie-Laure left the room.

"Your wife seems to be losing her shine," Henri commented to Ludovic. "Come with me; if we go crossing Sandra's room with a dog, it won't end well for us."

*Lord be thanked, I'm getting a divorce*, he thought. And, with Ganache at his heels, he went upstairs.

Ganache would have preferred to follow Ludovic or, of course, that other woman who was so gentle and sweetly scented, but Henri's glowering authority won out for this dog fleeing a rainstorm.

Ludovic and Fanny stayed quite still for a moment before both doubling over in sudden, unprompted laughter. They went out into the garden, sat for a moment on a bench a little way from the house, and, somewhat calmer, then joined by Philippe, they stayed to watch Henri's bedroom lights being turned off. At that precise moment, Sandra's window lit up again. Standing out in the darkness, the three were fascinated, delighted, and thoroughly tickled. Life had become life once more. They exchanged looks of affection, free of pity, and Philippe's face was quite magnanimous.

"If my sister discovers Ganache . . ." he said, slowly.

# 13.

It was at just that moment that an overjoyed Ganache barked his first bark into the night. The three listeners' laughter resounded so abundantly that their canine neighbors barked in answer to Ganache, and the barking redoubled along with the furious cries of a female person. It was in this moment of hilarity that Philippe saw Ludovic's hand resting on Fanny's hip. It was, therefore, at Ganache's first bark that he understood everything.

Philippe's intuition of the connection between Ludovic and Fanny seemed all the more conclusive in that only a dullard's inspiration and a bent for complications could have revealed it. That hand of Ludovic's wandering about the hips of his young mother-in-law in a moment of general distraction called more loudly to him than any flirtation, however gross. People, the public, society—in short, *others*—believe their intuitions all the more for being vague or any way different from their everyday impressions and regular fantasies: a sunlit kiss on the mouth can seem like a joke, but not a few words whispered in the night. On television and at the cinema we see dark ecstasy in all its unimaginable rawness. In real life we prefer surprising people to learning from them, much less understanding them. Often, we experience false impressions more sharply than true ones, as if the lie's horror clothes the false facts and makes them, in their very unlikeliness, the more undeniable.

What Fanny felt when she noticed Philippe's gaze could have been as much to her credit as her dishonor. In any case, she realized that she was inextricably connected to Ludovic, and she had neither the strength nor the indignation required to deny it. Whether the sky lit up or was blotted right out, the whole landscape had become fork-tongued: treacherous and particular.

The truth was there, between Ludovic's tweed and Fanny's silk dress. In their eyes on each other, the sexual truth that hung between them, never truly standing forth; in Quentin's death, Fanny's few lovers, the beaches, her flirtations and small pleasures, so threadbare ever since. And now, suddenly, a compulsive liar who got everything wrong was making her admit her desire, her irresistible attraction to a boy who thought himself completely in love with her, while she had never seen him in this light.

A boy with the courage of the straightforward, who loved what he desired, who was honest about what moved him, who—in short—surrendered unresisting to it all. Naïve, as no one else—or very few—had the openness, the courage, and the simplicity to be in this century.

Philippe's laugh had trailed off. Ludovic's, as if mysteriously aware, now grew more open, deeper, more masculine, gentler. And hers—what about her own laugh? It sounded worldly to her, false and lacking youth, lacking all connection with her two witnesses. Fanny's voice rang thin and ridiculous to her ear, just as her figure seemed to her. It was no longer of looseness or foolishness that she accused herself but cowardice. Ludovic's new laugh, his new voice, described virility—strength, decisiveness, and recklessness too—which was only the price of this desire, not a revelation of his nature, nor even one of his masks.

◆ ◆ ◆

All set for a long and sparkling evening, the next few hours shrank to fifteen minutes, thanks to Philippe's false discovery and Fanny's real one.

Ludovic alone was unperturbed. Even Fanny's step back from his shoulder had not shaken him. He had consolidated—he had won—he had put his finger on something between himself and her. Fanny had understood and accepted his feelings; she had slipped away from his tweed as if from a cocoon, her acceptance eternal, unaffected. He saw no connection with his brother—or indeed uncle—Philippe's gaze, for he seemed to Ludovic the incarnation of apathy and double dealing, although so prized by Sandra. Deluded and a liar but a good egg, *n'est-ce pas?*

Ludovic had hung on to quite a few old-fashioned expressions—idioms acquired at his boarding schools, enriched in the Parisian nightclubs, and, bizarrely, entrenched in the sanatoriums that followed. Ludovic would say: "good egg," or even "tip-top egg." He would exclaim: "There goes a lady," referring to her appearance, and "Now here's a real chap," as he strolled behind his industrialist father. It was some time since he had said anything of substance in praise of his wife, albeit "a rather spiffy person" when they first met. As for Sandra, she was "a lady of substance." Only Fanny escaped all descriptors, all qualification, all debate—a silence that, in this case, was quite the smartest move.

In the evening, "the children," as Sandra described Ludovic, Marie-Laure, Philippe, and Fanny, generally kissed each other on the cheek—one of those rare moments of instinctive rapprochement that the powerful, looming presence of such a lady of the house can inspire. Having emerged from infancy all unaware, adults may be united as much by fear and incomprehension as by solidarity. Except that evening, instead of kissing her cheek, Philippe kissed Fanny's hand, the hand of the new guilty party and so, to him, the newly respected object of singular drama in these lands so smothered in ease and ennui. And except that, as she kissed her young son-in-law's scrappily shaven cheek, Fanny's stiffness was visible to all around her. For Philippe this was further proof of her guilt, but for Ludovic, it was a chance to rest his lips on Fanny's sweet, scented cheek, fragrant with the perfume he'd first inhaled at Tours station and that, thereafter, he considered the only women's perfume there was.

That evening, Ludovic felt particularly young, happy, and in love, and, his timidity now practically snuffed out, his blindness about his own love seemed less complete than usual. His laugh likewise! "Laughter rides in with love," as somebody said, and indeed, there's nothing like laughter to cut morality down to size or even rub it right out. Letting go of Fanny's waist, which he'd automatically encircled, he lifted his arm and settled it now around her shoulders. Target sighted, he bent toward her, but her cheek was already too close; he had corralled her in by a height, a proximity that put him at her mouth level. Short of pushing her away or suddenly stepping back again, short of knocking forehead and chin together, the only possible solution consisted in lifting and turning her head very slightly, and her allowing herself to be kissed diagonally on the lips.

Which Fanny did allow, if only out of aesthetic concern, and which Ludovic did quite naturally, still under the hostile gaze of Philippe, who appreciated his role as psychological spy but not as disregarded witness. Besides, the kiss was very brief, for Fanny then turned on her heels, saying, "Oh, sorry," in a glacial voice. Philippe followed her, making a low, teasing whistle, and Ludovic followed Philippe.

# 14.

Sandra Cresson thought she'd heard a dog's bark and the clicking of four paws associated with her husband's commanding
tread as he crossed his bedroom. Instinctively, the idea of a dog
in his Louis XV suite made her giggle childishly.

"You know, Henri, I may be going mad," she said.

From the neighboring room Henri's voice rose in answer.
"Really?"

He sounded neither surprised nor upset. Of course, the
poor man had grown jaded. She propped herself up on her
pillows.

"I heard a dog barking, and then even crossing your room,"
she said, snorting with mirth.

"Now, now, my dear . . ."

"You'll swear blind that—"

"Quiet now, quiet! Come here and be quiet," said Henri.
"Stay on the bed and do be quiet!"

Effectively muzzled by Henri's words, especially their peremptory tone, Sandra did indeed fall silent; she was cut to the quick.

"Excuse me, my dear," came Henri's rather breathless voice again, "but . . . Come here, I say, here!"

"Goodness, Henri, you know quite well I can't walk at the moment, unfortunately."

"But who's asking you to walk? Err, do forgive me once more, Sandra. I'm pooped, and rather likely to have nightmares. I'll just close the door so you can sleep in peace."

And the sacred door, the one that always stood open between them and assured their double solitude, suddenly slammed shut. The bang was followed by the same clicking sound as before, a muffled, inexplicable clickety-click—unless Henri was practicing his tap dancing. But had he always been such a poor performer?

# 15.

Open, aired every day, and lined with all sorts of gorgeous clothes scattered about the floor, Fanny's room now had a countrified feel and a scent of mown grass, and the great plane tree's leaves slipping audaciously between the loose shutters revealed to her a dark-blue sky streaked with shooting stars, while the damp earth breathed its nightly softness upward.

Philippe had accompanied Fanny to her door, where he had kissed her hand with an enigmatic smile that she found maddening. He had said no more; tomorrow was another day for these comedies. So she crossed to the far side of her room, cast an uneasy, frustrated glance in the mirror, then went to look out the window. The great plane's leaves now lay all around her, sweet and rough like Ludovic's jacket . . . the roguish, impetuous, captivating Ludovic . . . the foolish boy who'd turned into a real man in the space of half a second, who had prevented her, with all her skills, from anticipating that shoulder, that arm, and that step forward or back, that graceless step back so that she could evade his mouth. And instead of shaking off Philippe's insistent eyes some other way, she'd spoken harshly to her lover, her unlucky son-in-law! As he let her go, he had once more touched her face, and had that awful Philippe not been leering so very close by they might perhaps still be together, just the two of them under that dizzy September sky.

There was a knock on the door. Fanny called, "Come in," imagining Philippe or Henri or Sandra with some foolishness. But it was Ludovic who, with boundless audacity, inched inside, a finger to his lips, conspiracy incarnate.

Shocked, Fanny nonetheless kept her voice low. "What are you doing here? Might it be to explain precisely how . . . ?"

She stopped, feeling ridiculous trying to reprimand this boy in his thirties, although she had never thought of or spoken to Ludovic as a mature man. Come to think of it, with whom *had* she done so, apart from Quentin? He would have laughed to see her there in her crumpled dress, fussing over her reputation in front of this young man fresh out of an asylum.

Ludovic had his tweed jacket over one arm; his hair was wild and his eyes sparkled. She was surprised she hadn't seen his beauty sooner. *For he is a handsome man, a very handsome man*, she conceded coolly. She had thought him a Billy Boy in shorts, but he stood before her a Prince Pushkin.

Out of habit, she nonetheless made him sit at the foot of her bed and, herself, sat on the other side. Ludovic's long legs rested on the carpet; Fanny sat with her own tucked up beneath her. What could she say that would not be hurtful?

"I don't want to humiliate my daughter, Ludovic," she began. "She is what she is, I grant you, but . . ."

"She is worse than that," Ludovic said, and looked down at Fanny's legs.

She tucked them up a little higher, nervously, finding the bedspread slippery and ugly, genuinely ugly.

Ludovic looked back at her and smiled without any guile. "It's always been like that," he said, "even when it was new. When I was little, my Aunt Marthe bought it for her wedding to Papa's older brother, André. André was killed in 1940, coming back here with their brother Marcel."

"How awful," said Fanny, disconcerted.

"And my father took over the factory when he was nineteen. He was the one who had that dreadful building put up in the valley, and here. But as he says: 'Dying in nineteen fourteen to eighteen made heroes of us, but in thirty-nine to forty, we were the suckers.' Excuse my . . . Both my aunts went home to their mothers filthy rich, but before leaving they wanted to make their mark. My mother came after that, but I never knew her and she didn't care about interior decor. And then, last of all, came Sandra, thanks to their shared land borders—a question of money, really—with my father."

"Poor Sandra . . ." Fanny was recovering her sense of perspective. "She's the most unhappy out of you all, here, don't you think?"

"No," Ludovic replied, firmly. "I used to be the most unhappy, but now I am the happiest."

"And why were you so unhappy?" she asked, severely, although Ludovic seemed not to notice.

"Nobody, no one at all, loved me or cared about me."

"Then couldn't you tell me all your childhood misfortunes tomorrow?"

Ludovic leapt up. Fanny slipped. He caught her and set her back on the bed like a doll. His white shirt lay open, showing his tanned neck, his glossy hair falling long over his collar; his chest, his mouth so wide and cool . . .

Fanny's memory must have been in utter disarray or quite off balance, for it sent her back into his arms, and her face was soon covered with long beseeching kisses, each one for her and for him alone. Their lips tasted each other's bodies, desire and devotion mingled, impulse and abandonment, faltering refusal and determined submission. All this in some strange way in this room sunk in darkness and translucence, where they trembled as wildly as the plane tree's leaves, as the sky and its spill of stars.

◆　◆　◆

When Fanny awoke, certain she couldn't have slept, the way it is after real nights of love, he had gone. She was furious for a moment at his disappearance, for his having left without saying anything, that he had dared to leave her. Upon which, yawning and stretching, she recognized those possessive signs of love. She told herself, "Of course, of course," in an effort to identify her feelings, and discovered nothing but well-being and her bodily weariness.

Fanny's sensuality was born of fidelity. Her wakings after Quentin had never been the same as waking with him, with the exception of this one, for the first time and so many years later, thanks to this mischievous kid of a man. She made no attempt to discover their precise difference in age, nor was she bothered about his marriage to her daughter, so far receded in her mind, nor that he'd been thought half-mad. She remembered that he'd said "I love you" because she had insisted that he hadn't been driving the doomed car on the day of his accident and that she, at least, remembered that. An "I love you" that he had not stopped saying, aloud and in whispers, since that night. What was a man who loved you if not his stubbled cheeks; his silences broken by inaudible, obvious words; this haste and this fear in equal measure?

She dressed with great care in a gown she knew had been made for her by a designer who disliked women but who could have claimed the opposite based on this gown alone. Yet she was reluctant to stand up, to abandon the mingled odors of

herself and her lover to the bathtub. And when she came down-
stairs to rejoin La Cressonnade for breakfast, she was neither
surprised nor put out by the many compliments she received.
In fact they amused her, being true and so quite pointless. And
she addressed no sweetheart smile to Ludovic, standing behind
his chair—golden, dark-haired, russet, almond eyes, half-open
mouth, body aslant, eyes rallying in the light of her gaze.

"What a woman!" exclaimed the man her own age, the Hawk
on High, the only person here whom she could have seduced
without creating a proper scandal.

"True enough," said Philippe, readily, for despite everything he liked women, and had had a fair few who'd appeared
dreamy over breakfast after his attentions. Nostalgia choked
him for a moment.

"She is in very good shape," said Marie-Laure, unambigu-
ous despite a sudden rush of jealousy.

"Absolutely!" Ludovic barked, in an impulse that could
have been incriminating had it not been patently sincere.

*She is mine*, he was reflecting. *She was naked in my arms
only two hours ago, and telling me* . . . Tears of gratitude, happiness, and pride rose to his eyes.

"After this, I'll be taking you to visit the caves at Saultes,"
Henri announced. Seeing their mystified faces, he added, "It's

Sunday and I've had the factory's Beechcraft brought over. I really ought to show Fanny the country around here. All she's seen so far are the shops."

"I do believe Fanny has seen the best of La Cressonnade," Philippe said with a smile so pointed that no one noticed the oddness of his statement, not even its object.

Indeed no threat could be made to stick now, after such a delicious pot of tea. What brand was it they used? Upon inquiry, Martin almost blushed to admit it was Lipton. In fact, and without realizing it, Fanny was making everyone blush that morning, in a great bittersweet wave, the way happy or fulfilled people sometimes do.

Fanny and Ludovic applied equal care to avoiding each other during the extremely odd flyover of the Touraine that Henri had concocted. This was a tour he had so far only offered the richest and dullest Japanese manufacturers of his acquaintance. They took two hours over it, including a fair few hundred jolts; the excursion would have taken half an hour by car. But the plane was Henri's secret weapon, even though the Hawk on High had never learned how to fly it—"Thanks be to Saint Christopher," as his relatives and subordinates put it.

Thus, Fanny spent a delightful and very strange day. The tour amused her; the fatigue of the night before and Ludovic's reassuring presence behind her warmed her face. Like many women of her age, Fanny looked to her lovers for protection, a notion quite antique to the next generation.

"How beautiful . . . how very beautiful," Marie-Laure said at her side, often to general surprise except to Philippe, who had noticed the tendency of deceived women—even those ignorant of their state—to play at little girls. Besides, she was right: castles, rivers, hills, the pale-blue sky, late summer; the Touraine rolled its charms out beneath them, and Henri's technical observations could do nothing to diminish them.

*How lovely France is*, Fanny was thinking, *and how beautiful my lover too . . .*

The plane smelled of the heather and satsuma orange bushes over which they flew so low, now and then, that they could breathe in the scent.

At one point, Fanny was struck by such potent desire, born of a particular memory of Ludovic, that she turned to him, then sat down again instantly before touching him with even a fingertip. This prohibition, the *impossibility*, was to be one of the most sensual memories of her life in love. And she upbraided herself, a moment later: *He is mad and I—I am perverse*, an idea that had never before occurred to her but that now arrived with the obviousness of those mistaken ideas we forge about ourselves when we're tired or riven with doubts. She looked at the shining eyes resting on her. She really would have had to hate him, truly hate him, in that moment, for his eyes to go out, to cloud over, for her to see a truer image of herself and him—that is, of a woman astray, far from Paris and in love with a great mooncalf gone half-crazy with loneliness.

# 16.

There were six days to go before the much-touted party, and everyone at the house was obsessed with the same question: Would Sandra be sufficiently stubborn to get up and make an appearance? This she had threatened everyone she would do, growing ever pinker in the face, despite Henri's imprecations.

Ludovic and Fanny met every night after days also spent together, and Philippe's nose was increasingly out of joint. But he understood that a horror of scandal outweighed curiosity in these circles. He also knew that Henri, himself captivated and unexpectedly gentlemanly so far, was liable to show him the door, and Philippe had experienced several similar situations that had ended very badly for those on hand (among which, himself), therefore . . .

In the end, the canniest of La Cressonnade's hosts turned out to be the dog, Ganache. At first drawn by the fragrance, the sweetness, and the femininity that Fanny embodied for him, he had rapidly realized his affections were shared—on occasion, at least—and that he could only ever come in second after that great scrawny man known as Ludovic, a fine runner deep down, and kind, but too distracted. The other two masters didn't even notice him. In fact, his only concern was avoiding the odd sly kick from Martin. No, the one true master he identified in this unexpectedly roomy lodging was the man with the voice like thunder, the one called Henri, who had the subtle sentimental power and authority proper for a master of the house, who was too often absent yet still manifestly the lord of these lands. Lord of all, except for that other animal kenneled, alas, in the room next door, a lady who sighed and made other strange new sounds. There lay the risk, and not for nothing had his master Henri taught him to avoid her den and instead to come in via the small hallway door to rejoin him in the evenings. It was only in the garden, on the terrace, and occasionally in his car that Henri would acknowledge their special relationship, calling Ganache "good old dustbin" or "my magnificent mutt," among other silly epithets which, in Henri's deep growl, warmed the dog's neglected heart. In that voice, alas, the creature discovered something like the human echo of his own call. They barked alike, but this only the perceptive Fanny had noticed.

# 17.

The heavens were having fun at their expense: either the sun was shining with a marmalade, autumnal light, or it was much too hot and oppressive, or it was raining and thundering. The weather would change radically about every two hours; the Touraine was starting to feel like Normandy. Both inside and outside the house, everything seemed to be vacillating. Only Ludovic was unstoppably there—Ludovic's gaze, his sweater, his hands, Ludovic's happiness—and Fanny could not avoid that, nor did she really wish to. It's one of the least difficult things to win a person's fascination or passion, but their happiness is the most difficult to secure if all you've actually done is watch and see them. Now, no one had ever looked at this boy with the idea of making his life a joy from start to finish. No one had wanted to fulfill him, entertain him, or make the most of him. Nor had anyone wished to cure him, either of an imagined madness or of his utter isolation. Fanny gave of her time, attention, and advice, and forgot herself completely.

The great tents erected along the terrace fluttered and soaked up rain and sun. Every day was the same, as was every night, for them both: as brief as they were essential. And yet, Quentin . . . Quentin. Who could she have loved, if not Quentin? In ten days the soirée would be over and Ludovic restored to respect (perhaps), and she would go back to her work and forget her reckless baby lover.

In her enormous country bed, Fanny found she was crying for no reason she could tell, while her lover slept. Crying with exhaustion, she told herself, stubbornly; they were tears of uncertainty, over some shadowy humiliation; tears of doubt. Ludovic never spoke of doubt or departure, nor of parting. And out of a kind of discretion, out of fear, she did not speak of these things either. Their gazes were as tightly entwined as their bodies, but at night, when he would light a cigarette for himself and one for her and they would whisper like teenagers too young to smoke, this was as much as they felt able to do.

For them the secret lay in the Ganache-Henri, Henri-Ganache love story, which had them in stitches and also meant they listened out, now and then, for the furthest room, for Sandra's raspy breathing and very manly snoring from the devious Philippe. So well-informed, he was, so discreet and so incensed. Marie-Laure's sarcastic comments to all and sundry grew ever more acerbic, but nobody was listening.

◆ ◆ ◆

At last the day of the great soirée came and, to everyone's surprise, it was a fine one. Like a gift, the sky began blue, stayed blue, and then darkened softly into black.

Gradually, the high society of Touraine, Paris, and everywhere else besides arrived in suitable vehicles to be parked in the field set aside for them. In their dinner jackets and evening dress, the various family members made an odd-looking bunch, all told. Henri had chosen between an outfit that was too tight and one that was too loose. Philippe had a single rather worn, though impeccably cut, suit from London, from his wild youth. As for Ludovic, he wore a dinner jacket that was now too big after his sanatoriums, but which looked good on him. His dark auburn hair and burnished eyes gave him an air of stability, and all this russet, this uprightness and shine, were concentrated in a shy smile that, after three mysterious years, now seduced both his kin and all his new friends at La Cressonnade. In fact, "like his mother, taken from us so young, he is auburn," as Henri said several times with the glowering pride of ignorance. Thirty years on, he was happy to concede that his young wife, his only love, had been auburn up until her death, even though he couldn't admit the very idea while she was alive, when he loved her; that he knew the silky dark chestnut of her hair by heart, in the times when he would bury his face in it sometimes in full view of everyone. Someone would mutter half to themselves: *when* he thought or *when* he was prompted to think of her. Some stuffed-shirt type, someone vaguely ridiculous, by Henri's lights, someone with no pride.

# ABOUT THE AUTHOR

Born in 1935 in Cajarc, a commune in the Lot department in France, Françoise Sagan spent her childhood in Paris and the years of the German occupation moving between Lyon and the Dauphiné region of the French Alps, where her father owned factories. She returned to Paris after the war to complete her schooling, after which she went on to study at the Sorbonne. It was there, over the summer of 1953, that she wrote *Bonjour Tristesse*. From the moment of its publication, the novel was a dazzling success. In 1956, her second novel, *Un certain sourire* (*A Certain Smile*), confirmed her status as a serious writer; this book, too, was a great success.

Sagan is generally described as having adopted a scandalous lifestyle; this fed into an image she struggled to escape thereafter—that of a habitué of casinos and nightclubs reveling in drink and fast cars. After a serious car accident in 1957, Sagan was left addicted to opioids following her recuperation.

Sagan published more than thirty books, including novels and short story collections, as well as nine plays (notably *Château en Suède*—*Château in Sweden*). She also cowrote a number of screenplays. In 1985 she was awarded Le Prix Littéraire for her lifetime's work. Financially and physically depleted, Sagan died in September 2004 in her house in Honfleur but was buried in the cemetery nearest to her native Cajarc.

Sagan wrote her own epitaph—her sense of her own style being, in her view, the mark of the true writer:

> *Made her entrance in 1954 with a slim novel, Bonjour Tristesse, which scandalized readers the world over. Her exit, after a life and oeuvre as pleasant and as botched as each other, was a scandal for none beside herself.*

Despite her outstanding debts, Denis Westhoff, Sagan's son from her second marriage, took on her estate and has chosen to fight for the posterity of her life's work. In 2020, he had her unfinished novel *Les quatre coins du cœur* (*The Four Corners of the Heart*) published and saw the foreign rights sold to fifteen countries. Françoise Sagan has thus been restored to her status as an icon and a key point of reference in French literature.

# ABOUT THE TRANSLATOR

Sophie R. Lewis is a translator and an editor. She is a Londoner by birth, and five years living in Rio de Janeiro provided her with some new loves. Working from Portuguese and French, she has translated Natalia Borges Polesso, João Gilberto Noll, Sheyla Smanioto, Stendhal, Jules Verne, Marcel Aymé, Violette Leduc, Leïla Slimani, Noémi Lefebvre, Mona Chollet, and Colette Fellous, among others. With Gitanjali Patel, she cofounded the Shadow Heroes translation workshops enterprise (www.shadowheroes.org).

Lewis's translations have been shortlisted for the Scott Moncrieff and Republic of Consciousness Prizes and longlisted for the International Booker Prize. She was joint winner of the 2022 French-American Foundation prize for nonfiction translation for her work on anthropologist Nastassja Martin's book *In the Eye of the Wild*.

# ABOUT THE TRANSLATOR